GEORGIANA DARCY'S DIARY

Jane Austen's *Pride and Prejudice* Continued

THE *PRIDE AND PREJUDICE* CHRONICLES

Georgiana Darcy's Diary
Pemberley to Waterloo
Kitty Bennet's Diary

GEORGIANA DARCY'S DIARY

Jane Austen's *Pride and Prejudice* Continued

ANNA ELLIOTT

with illustrations by Laura Masselos

a WILTON PRESS book

GEORGIANA DARCY'S DIARY
Jane Austen's *Pride and Prejudice* Continued

The cover incorporates a portrait of Rosamund Hester Elizabeth Croker painted in 1827 by Thomas Lawrence as well as a letter in Jane Austen's own hand. The title font is *Exmouth* from PrimaFont Software, and the date entries are set in the the font *Jane Austen* by Pia Frauss.

Illustrations are by Laura Masselos and are used with permission. The sketch depicting ladies around a table is based on "Young Ladies at Home" by Henry Moses, 1823, recreated by Laura Masselos in Georgiana's style.

Anna Elliott can be contacted at ae@AnnaElliottBooks.com. She would love to hear your comments.

ISBN-13: 978-0615609577
ISBN-10:   0615609570

 WILTON PRESS

for Jane Austen fans everywhere

AUTHOR'S NOTE

Of all the wonderful secondary characters in *Pride and Prejudice*, Georgiana Darcy has always been my favorite. In Jane Austen's original text, we never actually hear her speak a single direct word; any dialogue she has is merely summarized by the narrator. But to me, that only made her more intriguing. Just who was she, this painfully shy younger sister of the famous Mr. Darcy—a girl with a large fortune of her own, who at the age of fifteen was so very nearly seduced by the wicked Mr. Wickham?

Jane Austen herself gave her own family a few tidbits about what happened to her characters after the close of Pride and Prejudice. Kitty Bennet married a clergyman near Pemberley, while Mary married one of her uncle's clerks. But so far as is known, she never hinted at what happened to Georgiana Darcy after her brother married Elizabeth. For myself, I always felt that Georgiana Darcy ought to marry Colonel Fitzwilliam.

The modern reader may object that the two of them are cousins. But in Jane Austen's world, marriage between cousins wasn't considered at all improper—it was often absolutely encouraged. Queen Victoria married her first cousin Prince Albert of Saxe-Coburg and Gotha, and theirs was one of the happiest love stories and most famously successful marriages of the age. In fact, Jane Austen herself wrote about such romance in *Mansfield Park*: Fanny Price and Edmund Bertram are first cousins.

Of course, you'll have to keep reading to see whether, once I started writing their story, Georgiana and Colonel Fitzwilliam agreed with me that they were meant to be together!

I would especially like to thank the amazingly talented Laura Masselos, who provided original artwork for Georgiana's diary. Thank you, Laura! You truly captured exactly what I imagined Georgiana drawing, and brought her character's love for creating works of art to life.

One further note: I can't begin to match Jane Austen's immortal writing style, and wouldn't even pretend to try. That's one reason I chose a diary format for this story. I would never aspire to imitate Jane Austen or compare my work to hers. *Georgiana Darcy's Diary* is meant to be an entertainment, written for those readers who, like me, simply can't get enough of Jane Austen and her world.

Georgiana Darcy's Diary

Thursday 21 April 1814

At least I was not in love with Mr. Edgeware.

That sounds as though I am trying to salvage my pride, but I am truly not. I hate lying—especially to myself. And there is small point in keeping a private journal if I am only going to fill it with lies.

So, I was flattered by Mr. Edgeware's attentions. I liked him—or at least, I thought I did. But love? No.

Though I am sure my Aunt de Bourgh would say that is neither here nor there in considering whether Mr. Frank Edgeware and I should marry.

I don't seem to have begun this story at all properly. I have been keeping a diary on and off since I was ten, but I have not written an entry in a year or more. Maybe

I am out of practice with setting down the events of the day. I am not even entirely sure what made me pick up this notebook—a red leather-bound book of blank pages that Elizabeth gave me for Christmas. Except that the memory of what happened today feels like a festering sore inside me—and maybe writing it all down here will let the poison out.

To explain more clearly, then, Mr. Frank Edgeware is the youngest son of Sir John Edgeware of Gossington Park. Mr. Frank has been staying here at Pemberley for the last three weeks, one of the house party my aunt has imposed upon us all. He is a handsome man—really, a very handsome man, with dark hair and melting brown eyes and a sallow, lean kind of good looks.

Aunt de Bourgh—small surprise—has thrown us together a good deal, and he has been my partner at whist, has accompanied me for walks and rides about the grounds. We seemed to have so much in common, he and I. He would ask which poets I liked best, and when I mentioned Mr. Cowper, he would wholeheart-edly agree that Mr. Cowper's poems were masterpieces of language and feeling. The same with music. I spoke of Mr. Thomas Arne's operas, he professed himself a great lover of *Artaxerxes*, as well.

I can see now, of course, that I was an idiot to be so taken in. Anyone would think that after George Wickham's courtship, I would have learned to spot a fortune hunter. But at the time I had not a single suspicion that Frank Edgeware was anything but sincere.

Until this morning, when I chanced to be walking in the rose garden. I was on a path screened by a thick row of bushes and overheard Mr. Edgeware speaking to Sir John Huntington on the other side of the shrubs. They could not see me, of course, but I heard every word.

Sir John—he being another member of the house party, a goggle-eyed man with plump hands and greasy hair—asked Mr. Edgeware how he was progressing with Miss Georgiana Darcy.

And Mr. Edgeware laughed and replied that he fancied he would succeed in winning my hand in marriage, all right, and confidently expected to be wedded to me by the end of three months' time.

"And thank God that when we're wedded," he said, "I won't have to listen and pretend to agree while she maunders on about poets and musicians." He laughed again. "It's a good thing she has a fortune of thirty thousand pounds. She's a nice enough little thing, but ditchwater dull."

My whole body flashed hot and cold, and just for a second I wanted to smash my way through the bushes and confront the pair of them. But I did not. If I have not yet learned to judge men's characters, I at least know my own well enough. And I knew I would never in three hundred years work up the nerve for a dramatic confrontation of that kind. Or if I did, I would stand there, red-faced and stammering trying to to think of the perfect retort. Which would probably come to me at three o'clock the following morning, but not before.

Sometimes I hate being shy.

So I simply turned and walked—very quietly—away, before the men could guess they had been overheard.

Mr. Edgeware came to sit with me on the settee after dinner this evening, just as usual, and smiled into my eyes.

I wonder, now, that I never noticed how calculated his smile is. I can just imagine him practising it every morning in front of the mirror.

At any rate, he asked me whether I would consent to

play for the party this evening. He had been dreaming all day, he said, of hearing me play again on the pianoforte.

So I said that I had been practising a waltz by Mozart, and when he replied that he was absolutely enchanted with Mozart's waltzes, I smiled at him very sweetly. "Are you really?" I said. "They are nice enough, I suppose, but ditchwater dull."

It was some consolation, at least, to see the smile slide off his handsome face and the way he went red right to the tips of his ears. For once he had absolutely nothing to say; he just sat there, opening and closing his mouth like a fish out of water.

My affections truly were not engaged. It is only my pride that is hurt, not my heart. And really, Mr. Edgeware's deceit of me is incredibly petty when weighed against the other news of the day, which is that victory has been won over France at last.

Come to think of it, I really should have made that the opening of this journal entry, not the tag end; it's far more important than my own concerns. But—*peace*. It is such momentous news that I think everyone can scarcely take it in. Britain has been at war with France since before I was born—all eighteen years of my life— and I'd come almost to take it for granted. I think many people would say the same. But it's true—the latest word is that the Emperor Napoleon has been forced from his throne and is to be exiled. Our troops will be returning home.

I got all this from the newspapers, not from any note or letter of Edward's. I've not heard a single word from Edward since his regiment was called to foreign duty more than a year ago. Not since the last night I saw him, at the Pemberley Christmas ball.

But he can't have been killed—he can't. I've read the casualty lists in the papers every day, and his name has never appeared.

Still, I wish—

But I cannot write any more. It is very late. I am writing perched on the cushioned window seat, watching the moonlight glimmer on the lake in front of the house. My fingers are cramped with writing, and my ink is growing thin from being watered so often.

Friday 22 April 1814

It is a truth universally acknowledged that a young lady of rank and property will have packs of money- or land-hungry suitors yapping around her heels like hounds after a fox.

I said as much to Elizabeth this morning, when we were looking over my new gown for the ball next month, which had just arrived by special delivery from London.

Elizabeth laughed and said she quite liked that comparison, because she could imagine my aunt, Lady Catherine de Bourgh, as a huntswoman, cheering on the packs of suitors with cries of *Yoiks!* and *Tally-ho!*

But then she stopped laughing and said, looking at me, her gaze serious for once, "There's no one among the young men staying here you like, Georgiana? Truly? Mr. Folliet? Or Mr. Carter, even?"

I hung up the gown we had been examining in the wardrobe. It is very pretty: pale peach silk with an overdress of cream-coloured gauze, all embroidered with tiny rosebuds. And I am sure I would like it even more were it not further evidence that my aunt has determined to see me married within the year, it being a scandal that any niece of hers should have reached

the age of eighteen—and had two Seasons in London—
without being at the very least engaged.

"None," I said. "Or rather, I like some of them.
But not *that* way. I don't wish to marry any of them.
Unless—" I stopped as a thought struck me coldly. "Does
my brother . . . does he wish that I should?"

"Of course not! Not unless you want to, that is."
Elizabeth tilted her head to look at me from where she
was perched on the edge of my bed. "Georgiana, you
cannot truly think he would allow you to be pushed
into a marriage just to please your aunt?"

"Yes—I mean, no, I do not think that."

Elizabeth said, "Listen to me. Darcy agreed to this
house party scheme of Lady Catherine's because he
worries—as I do!—that you go out too little into society. That you have small chance of meeting any nice,
agreeable young men. But that is all." She watched me
for a moment, her dark eyes thoughtful. Then she said,
"You could speak to him, though, if you truly hate all
this so much." She smiled. "He doesn't bite, I promise
you. He wouldn't even be angry."

"I know." I *do* know. I think. It is just that my brother
Fitzwilliam is eleven years older than I am. And he has
been my guardian since I was ten years old.

He has been such a good brother to me. But I think I
am a little in awe of him, still.

More than a little.

And I know I have already given him far more worry
than he deserves.

"But it's all right," I told Elizabeth. "It's just . . . that
I'm *happy* here. I love it here at Pemberley with you.
Unless—" My whole body flashed hot and cold all over
again. "Unless you feel I'm in the way? If you'd prefer
to have the place to yourselves, without your husband's

unmarried sister—"

"Of course not!" Elizabeth said. "Of *course* I don't feel that."

It seems strange, now, to think that I almost dreaded my brother's marrying Elizabeth. Not that I did not like her—because I did like her very much, right from the first time I was introduced to her. It was just that she was a stranger, moving into our family and our home. At least, that was how it felt to me at the time.

I have always hated change. I think maybe it started when my mother died—but now and for as long as I can remember, I have felt a sick, hollow feeling every time a round of changes comes. When I was first sent away to school—and then again when I had to leave. Even last year, when a storm blew down the oldest and tallest of the Spanish oaks on Pemberley's lawn, I felt so grieved, silly as I knew it was.

But Elizabeth is not at all a stranger anymore—she feels almost like the sister I used to wish for when I was small. And—though it seems disloyal to say it—I can speak to her much more easily than I can to my brother.

"I was just saying to Darcy," Elizabeth went on, "that it's his responsibility to vet your potential suitors for me—no men allowed who live at more than a day's travel from here, because if you married and went too far away, I'd break my heart missing you. I'd be perfectly happy to keep you here with us always. But—"

Elizabeth broke off. "Oh, well—haven't you ever noticed the abominable habit newly married people have of wishing to see all their friends married, as well?" She spoke lightly. But all the same there was a look on her face that made me feel suddenly lonely. The way I feel sometimes when I see her and Fitzwilliam catch each other's eyes and smile at each other.

They have been married for just over a year, now, and they're so happy together it fairly hovers like a sunburst all around them; you can't be in the same room with them and not realise how deeply and sincerely attached to each other they are.

Even my Aunt de Bourgh has stopped resenting my brother's marrying Elizabeth quite so much. Though of course for my aunt, that means merely that she waits until Elizabeth is out of the room to speak of 'my nephew's unfortunate marriage' in the same tones you might hear at a funeral.

Elizabeth only laughs, though, and says she's glad, for it gives her the upper hand and makes Fitzwilliam feel he is lucky she consented to marry him, despite his horrible relations.

"Mr. Edgeware looked quite bereft last night," Elizabeth went on. "When you asked me to turn music pages for you at the pianoforte instead of him."

"I imagine he did." And then I told Elizabeth what had happened, everything of what I had overheard Frank saying in the garden to Sir John.

Elizabeth has been looking a little pale and tired, lately. Or tired for her. But her cheeks flushed bright scarlet at that, and she looked furious. She laughed, though, when I told her of my revenge, and she said, "Oh, well done! Exactly what he deserved." Which—almost—took the sting away from the memory.

Then she hugged me again and said, "You're not dull—and anyone who thinks you are is a blind fool and doesn't deserve you. But Georgiana"—she looked at me—"never mind your aunt's contenders, are there no other young men you might like? You're not"—all of a sudden her eyes went wide and alarmed—"you're not still in love with Mr. Wickham, are you?"

I smiled at that. Even if the smile tasted bitter on my lips. "Good heavens, no. I promise you, whatever else I am, I'm not in love with Mr. George Wickham."

Elizabeth let out her breath. "Well, thank goodness for that, at least. But . . . but there's no one else? Truly?"

I swallowed. And then I shook my head. Perhaps if I had grown up with four sisters as Elizabeth had I might find confidences easier.

But as it was, my throat closed up and my palms went clammy at even the thought of telling Elizabeth that there *was* someone else. I have never spoken of it to anyone, not ever. But there is Colonel Edward Fitz-william, the man I have been in love with since I was six years old.

Saturday 23 April 1814

I'm sitting-up in bed with the candle on my night table lighted and flickering beside me. It has stopped raining at long last, but I can hear the wind outside howling in the chimneys.

All the rest of the house is asleep, even my Aunt de Bourgh. She sleeps poorly and is often wakeful until past midnight. But I have just heard her long-suffering maid Dawson go past my door on her way to the ser-vants' wing and her own bed, so my aunt must be truly settled now. My aunt keeps Dawson until late most nights, making her read from a book of sermons and rub her back until she can drop off.

Two things happened today.

The first was a letter from Edward. Though it was sent to my brother, not to me.

Fitzwilliam had been up and riding out early to con-sult with his farm bailiff about the spring planting. But he came in for breakfast and opened the letters piled beside his place at the table. When he got to Edward's, I felt my heart jump, because of course I recognised the handwriting on the envelope.

It seemed an eternity before he looked up at Elizabeth and said, "It's from Edward. He says he has been wounded and granted a leave of absence, and would like to spend it here."

I gasped despite myself and Elizabeth gave a little cry of distress and said, "Wounded? Oh, no, poor Edward, is he seriously hurt?"

My brother glanced through the letter again and said, "He says it's nothing much, just a musket ball in his shoulder. He took it at Toulouse, he says—just before it was announced that Napoleon had surrendered."

And Elizabeth said, "That does not signify. Men always lie about how badly they're hurt, and soldiers are worst of all. But if he is well enough to write and to travel, he can't be too badly injured."

I did not say anything. My heart was beating too quickly and too hard.

I read of the battle for Toulouse in the newspaper reports. Nearly five thousand British and allied soldiers were killed. And the French lost three thousand of their own.

And all for nothing, too—because Napoleon had abdicated four days before the battle occurred. If only word had reached Toulouse in the South, all those lives might have been spared.

Still, as Fitzwilliam spoke, I drew what felt like my first breath in all the time Edward has been gone. He may have been wounded. But his letter shows that he survived the fighting, and now he's coming *home*.

The second event—

I suppose today's second occurrence is what is keeping me awake tonight. Even more than Edward's letter.

A travelling band of gypsies came to the house and offered to entertain us and tell fortunes after supper.

My aunt looked as horrified as though she had uncovered a dish at dinner and found a plate of wriggling worms instead of pork cutlets. But Elizabeth had already gone to the window and looked out and seen them grouped around the front door. They looked poor and wet and miserable and there were several little children without any shoes, their feet almost blue with the cold.

Elizabeth turned to my brother and said, "Please, Darcy." And my brother nodded and said, "Very well, let them come."

I truly did wish, then, that I was more like Elizabeth. I had thought of slipping up to my room when no one was watching and finding some money to give to them. But I should never have been bold enough to speak up in front of everyone as she did.

The music was beautiful in a wild, lilting way. One of the men played a fiddle and some of the women played tambourines and danced. And then one of the oldest, a little, wizened old woman with a dirty red scarf wrapped around her head and with her body swathed in so many shawls one could scarcely see her shape, offered to tell fortunes.

She turned to my cousin Anne first and asked if she would like her fortune told, and Anne sat up and looked quite bright and interested. But then, of course, she looked at her mother. My aunt could not quite bring herself to look at the old gypsy woman directly, but she sniffed through her nose and said, "Anne, you are going to have a headache. You must go up to your room at once and go to bed. I will send Dawson to you with some barley water for you to drink."

If I am honest—which I suppose I have, after all, resolved to be—I will say that I have never managed to like my cousin Anne very much. *No one* could really like my cousin Anne. My aunt decided when she was a child that Anne was of a sickly disposition. Whether it is true or not, I do not know. I have never known Anne to be really ill—not with any identifiable malady, at least, nor even a serious one.

But Aunt de Bourgh has convinced Anne herself of her poor health so completely that Anne does nothing but sit in the warmest place in a room, smothered in lap rugs. She scarcely ever speaks, save to talk in a dull, colourless voice of the pains in her head or her eyes or her lungs—or whatever other part of her Aunt de Bourgh has decreed is feeling poorly that day.

Tonight, I stood up and said, "Anne, we could go and have our fortunes told together, if you'd like. You needn't go alone."

But all the life and colour had already gone out of Anne's face as my aunt looked at her, and she only muttered something indistinguishable and drooped upstairs to bed.

So I went over on my own to the small table where the old gypsy woman had set herself up in a corner of the room.

Seen up close, the old woman's face was wrinkled and leathery as a dried apple, and her eyes were rheumy. Her hands were big, though—gnarled with age, but almost as strong-looking as a man's. And she took my hand in one of hers and looked into my palm.

"Ah." She drew in her breath and looked up into my face, nodding and bobbing her head. She had a cracked voice and spoke almost in a sing-song manner. "A happy future here, no question of that. I see a man coming into your life, my dear. He will be handsome and brave and strong and kind and wealthy, very wealthy, and—"

I suppose I was still feeling angry with my aunt, and impatient with Anne for never standing up to her, because I interrupted the old woman before she could say any more. "Hadn't you better stop while you're ahead?" I asked. "There aren't all that many more nice, promising-sounding adjectives you can use to describe this mysterious gentleman."

The old gypsy blinked at me for a second. And then she threw back her head and laughed. Her speaking voice might be cracked, but she had a nice laugh, throaty and full.

"Ah," she said again. And then she peered more closely into my face. "Most girls I give fortunes to—" She hawked and spat right onto the carpet, which I am sure gave my aunt fits if she was watching. "Empty-headed little dolls. They want to hear nothing but that they will meet a man. A handsome man, very rich." She closed one eye in a wink. "Usually pay extra if I tell them they'll be married within the year."

I laughed at that. I found myself liking the old woman despite myself.

"But you—very well, you I will give a real fortune." She took my hand again and looked into my palm, her whole face twisted this time into a fierce scowl of concentration. "You are strong. Stronger than you think, and with more courage than you believe yourself to have." Her voice was no longer sing-song, but somehow it still sent a trickle of cold down my spine. "I see a change ahead for you. A change in your life, in yourself." She closed her eyes in another wink. "I will not argue if you pay me extra, you understand. But this I would tell you in any case. You do not trust or love lightly—you do not believe you can trust your own heart or your own eyes to tell you true." She folded my fingers over my palm and squeezed my hand, her rheumy eyes still on my face. "But I think you may trust your heart from now on, for this I will say: I see love. I see an old love returning to you, and very soon."

Sunday 24 April 1814

It has occurred to me that perhaps I should have begun this journal by introducing the members of our house party properly and one at a time. Of course, no one reads this diary but me—but one never knows. Maybe some members of a future generation will come across it one day in a musty old trunk and waste countless hours trying to puzzle out who everyone is. So for the sake of my imaginary great-grandchildren—or maybe great-nieces and -nephews—I will set full descriptions of each guest at Pemberley down here and now.

Besides, it is raining again, so that we are trapped in the house for the morning. I am longing to practice the pianoforte—but not with such an audience about. I am always too nervous of making mistakes to concentrate on the music when there are too many people listening to me play.

And more importantly, the instant I stop writing, my Aunt de Bourgh will begin her inevitable scolding because I only played last night and didn't join the others in dancing. Elizabeth said she was feeling a bit tired and not up to dancing, so she sat beside me and turned the pages. I hope she's not unwell. She looks a little pale again today, and when I sat next to her at breakfast, I noticed she took only some dry toast and ate scarcely a mouthful of that.

At any rate, the house party: Firstly, there are my brother, Mr. Fitzwilliam Darcy, and his wife, Elizabeth. Though perhaps they don't count, because they live at Pemberley year-round. Still, I said I would describe everyone, and they make for an easy place to begin.

My brother is eleven years older than I am, which makes him nine-and-twenty this year. He is tall, with dark hair and dark eyes. He is very handsome—if I can say that about my own brother.

I remember when I was small, he seemed so very grown-up to me. He had already left the schoolroom before I even entered it, and by the time I was four, he was already off at school and only came home on holidays. I used to love those times. He would always bring a present for me—a doll or a hair ribbon or sugared lemons—when he came home. And I remember when I was very little—two or three, maybe—and visitors would come to call, he would always carry me around on his shoulder, because I was too shy to speak to anyone.

But of course there was too great a difference in our ages for us to be close confidants.

Our mother died when I was six. And then when I was ten, our father died, as well. Fitzwilliam was left to become my guardian—and to run the estate at Pemberley. The park and the timber and all two hundred tenant farms.

He felt the responsibility very keenly, I know. He had always been sober and serious, and after that he grew even more so.

He did make sure I was happy at school—and he always came home with me to Pemberley or to the

London house when there was a school holiday. But I did not wish to worry him with my concerns, so I cannot say I ever spoke to him very much of how I felt.

And now—now he is still a truly good brother. And since he and Elizabeth have been wedded, he smiles and laughs far more than he used to. But I still . . . I don't know. Perhaps he still thinks of me a little as the ten-year-old girl that suddenly became his responsibility to be almost a father for.

And I know that with him, I still feel at least in small part like a child in the schoolroom, looking up at the grown-up's world. Even if I am now eighteen.

Elizabeth is my brother's wife. Though of course I said that already, didn't I?

She was Elizabeth Bennet before she married him, of Longbourn in Hertfordshire. Elizabeth has dark hair and creamy pale skin. She has lovely dark eyes, though she is not a great beauty—at least to anyone who first meets her. But somehow the moment she smiles and starts speaking, she is beautiful. She can light up a room just by coming into it and charm anyone from the boy who cleans the knives and boots all the way up to an elderly duke.

I would not trade places—I suppose we none of us really want to be anyone but ourselves. But if I am being truthful, I do sometimes wish I could be more like her. Light and bright and sparkling and never seeming to worry over knowing the right thing to say or what other people will think of her.

I think Edward—Colonel Fitzwilliam—was a little in love with her before she married my brother. But of course, Edward is the younger son of an earl, which means he's expected to marry both position and fortune. Though I asked Elizabeth about him once—it was last year when we were afraid he might be sent off to fight in the Americas—and she said that she liked Edward very much, but that if he had been really in love with her, her lack of fortune would have mattered as little to him as it did to my brother.

But I am wandering off the subject.

Caroline Bingley, the sister of my brother's friend Charles, is staying with us for a while, since Charles' wife—Elizabeth's sister—Jane is confined with the birth of their first child.

Caroline dresses in bright colours and heavy, stiff brocades, and is handsome in a tall, imposing way, with dark-blonde hair and blue eyes, like a picture of a Viking maiden I once saw in a book. She and I are friends, of a sort.

Which means that before my brother married Elizabeth, Caroline hoped desperately to marry him herself. And she tried her hardest to ingratiate herself with me as a way of growing closer to him.

That sounds as though I resent her for it—and maybe I did at the time.

Caroline is the kind of girl I am always a little afraid of—or at least intimidated by. She has a strong voice and very decided opinions, and a very sharp tongue when she is speaking of anyone she dislikes—of which there are many.

I used to hate it when she would gush praises over my sketch work and my pianoforte playing, because I knew perfectly well that she would have never said two words to me if I had not been Mr. Fitzwilliam Darcy's younger sister. And I never knew what to say in return to her compliments, because I would keep imagining the things she probably said about me behind my back.

My thanks always sounded so chilly and stilted in

comparison to her (albeit insincere) words that I would feel suddenly conscious and more intimidated by Caroline than ever—and that would make me sound less friendly even than before.

Now, though—now Caroline seems to me a little like a child's balloon toy that's been pricked and had the air let out of it. That my brother could truly have fallen in love with Elizabeth instead of with her has left her shaken, I think, as though the ground under her feet has shifted and tipped and she is not quite sure now where she stands.

I found her just the other day standing in the morning room and looking up at herself in the mirror over the mantle with her hands clenched and her eyes filled with tears. And when she heard me behind her she whirled round and clutched my hand and said, "I'm handsome, Georgiana, aren't I?"

I was startled—for I had never seen Caroline cry before. But I said, "Of course you are, Caroline. But you scarcely need me to tell you that, do you? Not when you have both mirrors and men."

Caroline scrubbed at her eyes and said, "I mustn't cry. It makes me look a fright. It's only . . . I'll be four-and-twenty on my next birthday, and I always thought I'd be married by now. Married and with a home and children of my own, just like my brother and Jane are going to have."

Since then, she has seemed a little more in control. But still, I'm sure she wishes the men of the party were taking more of an interest in her.

And speaking of the men, there are four gentlemen staying here at Pemberley.

Or rather, we had four until yesterday, when Mr. Edgeware abruptly remembered a previous engagement elsewhere. I have no more faith in his engagement than in his professed admiration of Mozart. But I am relieved that I need not meet with him again.

So now there are only three men here, besides my brother.

Sir John Huntington I suppose I have already described, but for the sake of completeness I'll put him down again here. He is of course well born, or my aunt would not have considered him a contender for my hand. He has prominent gooseberry-green eyes and small, plump hands and greasy reddish brown hair and so far I have heard him speak of nothing but playing cards and horses. But I suppose to be fair I should not hold that against him, he may be very nice.

Except that he laughed at what Mr. Edgeware said about me. Which means that if he has a nice disposition under all the greasy hair and talk of horses, he will be a hundred years old before I ever find it out because I would rather chew on rusty nails than ever speak to him again.

The other two gentlemen I've spoken to scarcely at all, since they only arrived here at Pemberley four days ago. One is the Honourable Mr. Hugh Folliet, who is the grandson of the Earl of Cantrell. The old earl's daughter, Mr. Folliet's mother, and Aunt de Bourgh were at school together years ago, which is how Mr. Folliet comes to be staying here.

He looks to be about twenty-five, or a few years more. He has dark hair and dark eyes and he's very handsome—really, one of the most handsome men I've ever seen, like a knight in an old romance. Sir Lancelot, maybe, if Lancelot wore buckskin breeches and stiff white cravats.

The other gentleman is Mr. Carter, a friend of my

brother's from his school days. And he, at least, is certainly not one of my aunt's candidates, because he is a clergyman, and quite poor to judge by the threadbare collar of his coat and the cracked soles of his boots. But I like him—or at least I like what I've seen of him. He has sandy fair hair that is forever flopping down over his forehead into his eyes and he speaks with a slight stammer. But he looks thoughtful and intelligent, and I think he must be kind, as well. The other night my cousin Anne was sitting huddled by the fire as usual, and he sat down next to her and stayed there speaking with her for quite some time. Her usually sallow cheeks flushed with the heat of the fire and she smiled very often at whatever he said and really looked quite pretty.

I suppose that actually I have given a fairly complete sketch of my cousin Anne already, without entirely meaning to. But for the sake of completeness, I will put her down again here. She is my brother's age, or nearly so—she will turn twenty-nine in July. But she looks far younger because she is so very thin and small. Her hair is fair, straight and baby-fine, and she has a small, pale face that might be pretty if she did not always look so querulous and cross.

She must be horribly bored, though, so I can't really blame her for being petulant at times. My aunt never allows her to read, for fear of straining her eyes, never allows her to ride or go out for a walk for fear of taking a chill. She's not even allowed to embroider or paint or play the pianoforte for fear the effort will over-tire her.

I think I have mentioned it before, but my aunt is Lady Catherine de Bourgh. She is the daughter of my grandfather the earl, and the widow of Sir Lewis de Bourgh. She is—

How strange, I have known her all my life, but I have

never thought about how to describe her before.

Aunt de Bourgh is a tall woman with a square-built, broad-shouldered frame. She never speaks of her age, but I should think she must be fifty, or perhaps a year or two more. She has bold, strongly marked features and dark hair threaded with grey that she wears piled atop her head, and she speaks with a deep voice, very loud and very firm.

I don't suppose anyone could have read the past few entries in this diary without realising that my aunt is exceedingly proud and likes to order other people's lives for them. And she likes to have things her own way. I was terrified of her when I was a child—I can just remember hiding behind my mother's skirts one of the first times I was taken to visit her at Rosings Park, her estate. I can still see my aunt peering down her nose at me and booming out, "Upon my word, you seem to have entirely neglected to teach the child proper manners."

I suppose I must still be frightened of her—otherwise I would simply have told her straight out that I do not wish to marry any of her parade of suitors.

And yet . . . I don't quite know what it is I want to say. Save that it sometimes seems to me that anyone who makes other people as miserable as she does cannot be very happy herself.

And that makes up the whole of our house party here at Pemberley. I wonder if any of my subjects would recognise themselves if they read these descriptions without the names attached. I've never taken anyone's likeness in just words before. It is more difficult than I thought.

I think I'll try it with a picture, next. Here are all of the ladies in the morning room this morning, whiling away the hours and hoping the rain won't last all day.

Elizabeth is standing next to my cousin Anne. My Aunt de Bourgh comes next and then Caroline Bingley. And I am at the back, writing in this book.

Monday 25 April 1814

I've just realised—perhaps I should have begun first of all by describing myself? That seems a little strange in my own private journal. But I suppose those future descendants I was imagining would want to know who I am?

At any rate, I shall see if I can write a character sketch of myself here—if only because it seems only just, since I have done everyone else.

My full name is Georgiana Catherine Anne Darcy. Georgiana after the King, Catherine after Aunt de Bourgh, and Anne for my mother. I am eighteen years of age. My parents died when I was small, leaving me to the care of my brother and my cousin, Edward

Fitzwilliam. Though my brother is only eleven years older than I am, and Edward ten.

I am tall for a girl and slightly built—though thankfully not as spindly-legged and skinny as I was as a child. I have very dark hair—almost black, like my brother's—and dark eyes.

This is sounding very brief and stiff, isn't it? My hypothetical descendants will be thinking Mr. Edgeware was right, and I really am the dullest person alive.

I suppose it's even harder to write of myself than it was the others—all the more because I have never tried before.

I wonder what more I can say, though? That my fortune—left to me by my father—is thirty thousand pounds?

At the moment, I feel rather as though I should like to forget all about it.

I suppose I could claim accomplishment—but of course any girl would do that. Every young lady must be accomplished: paint and draw and play on the pianoforte—and execute embroidered needlework to perfection, as well. Because those are the skills gentlemen wish in a wife, and to attract a good match, we must all be sure to acquire them.

Which seems strange to me. In the entire history of the world has any man, anywhere, honestly cared about an embroidered landscape picture? Much less passionately desired that his wife be able to cover the walls of his home with them?

Still, after my father died, I was sent away to school and taught all the usual accomplishments just like the other girls.

I suppose this is exactly what any girl *would* say—though maybe it is more believable since I am only writing it down here in these private pages? Since I cannot worry too terribly about what my imagined great nephews and nieces think of me—but I really do love to play the pianoforte. I have been told I'm quite good at it, too—even by Miss LeFarge, our school music mistress, who had the worst breath I have ever encountered and disliked everyone, including me, on general principle.

I like to sing, too—though I like it far more when I am alone than I do performing in public.

And I love to draw, too. And that I actually *can* prove, since it is easy enough to include drawings in these pages.

And now that we have returned to Pemberley from the London house, I love to walk in the hushed stillness of the woods here, and watch the way the mother birds push their chicks from the nest when they are ready to fly, and see the morning dew glinting on the spider's webs and try to capture in crayon and paper the way the cat-tail reeds by the lake look when they have gone to downy seed.

Tuesday 26 April 1814

Mr. Goulding, our old parish clergyman, would call such sentiments heretical, but it seems to me that Fate has a strange sense of humour at times.

Even here, alone in my little sitting room, my toes are curling at having to write this down. But despite myself I did—I will admit it—believe just a little bit in the old gypsy woman's fortune. She spoke of seeing an old love returning. And on that very morning, a letter had arrived from Edward, saying that he would be visiting Pemberley in a week's time.

I know such prophesies are nonsense, of course. And yet—very well, I will admit this, too—all the time I was lying awake the other night, I was spinning equally nonsensical fairy tales in my imagination. Edward, seeing me in the garden on the day of his arrival and suddenly realising that I am not a child anymore. Sweeping me into his arms and murmuring broken endearments the way the heroes do in sentimental novels.

My skin is crawling with embarrassment just reading that on paper.

But this morning, Elizabeth received a letter from her sister Kitty, who is recently engaged to be married to a captain in Edward's regiment.

My aunt and cousin are taking breakfast in their rooms, and since the rain has stopped, Caroline Bingley has gone out to take a ride around the lake with some of the men. Elizabeth and I were sitting here in my sitting room alone while she read her letters and I—finally—took the chance to play the pianoforte, for I never mind Elizabeth hearing me practice.

But then, all at once, Elizabeth said, "Oh!" in a surprised voice.

I stopped playing and looked around and asked her whether something was wrong. "Is there bad news?"

Elizabeth shook her head. "No—quite the reverse. It is good news. Or at least I hope it is. Kitty writes to say that she hears from John"—John is Kitty's betrothed—"that Colonel Fitzwilliam is engaged to be married."

Elizabeth glanced down at the letter again—which I was thankful for, because it meant she was not looking at me. "To a Miss Mary Graves, so Kitty says. She says that he met Miss Graves in London last year, just before the regiment departed for France."

I swallowed. "Does she"—I was surprised, but my voice sounded almost normal, if a little distant in my own ears—"does your sister give any particulars about Miss . . . Miss Graves?"

Elizabeth shook her head. "No. You know Kitty. Or rather, I suppose you don't, not really, for you've only met her once. But believe me, she's not the most conscientious of correspondents. She only gives the news about Edward and then goes on to write about all the wedding clothes that she's having made." She stopped and shook her head again, still looking down at the letter. "Edward is such a dear. I'll be so happy for him—if only this girl is truly worthy of him, and he's sincerely attached to her."

I said something. I have no idea what it was I said— but it must have been some sort of appropriate words of agreement, because Elizabeth nodded. Then she said she must speak to Mrs. Reynolds, our housekeeper, about tonight's menu for dinner and went out, leaving me alone.

I have not cried. I am not going to cry. I have already been idiot enough for one day, and I would lose my self-respect entirely if I sat here weeping over this news.

Maybe the old love the gypsy woman told me was going to return was my little cat, Frederick, who ran away and was lost when I was eight.

All right, I would be happy to see Frederick again.

And maybe I will take one look at Edward and realise that what I felt for him was only a child's infatuation. It has been a year since I've seen him—maybe he has grown bald. Or fat.

Though I have a horrible, sinking feeling inside me that it would not matter to me if he had.

Wednesday 27 April 1814

I grew up with Edward almost as another older brother, but I have not seen him in more than a year. Not since his regiment left to serve under Sir Arthur Wellesley in the Sixth Coalition against the Emperor Napoleon.

Of course, most commissioned army officers never actually serve in the army—not to see battle, I mean. They most often live in London, where they are very fashionable men-about-town. And those with large enough private incomes usually agree to go on half-pay, which means that they are not even required to spend time with their regiments or perform any duties save for purely ornamental ones.

I am sure Edward's father expected Edward would be exactly that kind of officer, when he purchased a commission for him. But then when I was twelve, Edward's regiment was called to foreign service to defend Portugal against the French army. And he has fought with his regiment ever since.

Eighteen months ago, he was home in Britain for several months during a lull in the fighting. He was home for Elizabeth and my brother's wedding a year ago at Christmastime, and he came to stay at Pemberley for Christmas, along with Elizabeth's Uncle and Aunt Gardiner.

That was the last I saw him, at the dance my brother held in the Gardiners' honour.

Actually, there was such a crowd of guests that I scarcely saw him all that night—not until late in the evening when I was dancing with Sir John Dalrymple. Sir John is—again small surprise—one of my aunt's favourite contenders for my hand. I suppose I should count myself lucky that he is not a guest here at Pemberley now.

Though that is not quite fair to Sir John. He is a nice young man—or rather, there's no malice in him. It's just that he is loud and red-faced, has absolutely no sense of humour, and is a devoted lover of food. He is almost as broad as he is tall, with soft, doughy features and plump hands. He does not speak so much as bellow—and all through the dance he could talk of nothing but his new French cook. By the time the dance finished, he had enumerated each dish the new cook had made for him, one by one.

I was just about to thank him and make my escape, but Sir John kept tight hold of my hand. "I'm sorry," he said. "I'm not much used to talking to girls. I expect I've been boring you silly."

He looked so crestfallen that I said, quickly, "Oh, no! It's been very interesting. Um, *ragout of pullets and sweetbreads*, did you say?"

Which was a mistake, because Sir John brightened at once and said, "I hope you'll give me another dance?"

And that stopped me, of course. I had not the heart to refuse—how could I, without hurting his feelings? But before I could utter a word, Edward was there next to me, bowing formally to Sir John.

"You'll excuse me, Dalrymple," he said. "But as Miss Darcy's guardian, I can't possibly allow her to dance more than one dance with a single gentleman."

Edward was wearing his army uniform: red coat and white breeches. He is tall and broad-shouldered, and he made an impressive figure, with his brows drawn and his lean face stern and grim. Sir John certainly thought so. He blanched, swallowed visibly, bowed and then beat a hasty retreat.

I turned to Edward to thank him, but he was looking at me, his mouth twitching at the corners as he shook his head. He must have heard the whole of Sir John's and my final exchange.

"Am I going to have to give you lessons in saying no? Just to prevent my coming home to find you married to the first crashing bore who asks, just because you're afraid of hurting his feelings?"

"I wouldn't have married him!" I protested. But Edward was already shaking his head and pulling me from the dance floor.

"No. Not another word. I've been watching you all night. First you danced with Lord Waterstone, who's a spineless fop. Then Gerald Cartright, who dances as though he's got two left feet. And now Dalrymple. You're going to learn to stand up for yourself if it kills me."

No one would call Edward handsome. Not exactly. His features are too lean, too angular for that. But he has a *good* face. Strong and dependable, with humour in the set of his mouth and in his deep-set dark eyes. His hair is dark, too, and falls over his brow.

He pulled me with him into the hallway outside the ballroom. No one was there, save for ourselves. The guests were all dancing or talking inside, and the servants were all busy with laying out the supper things.

"All right," Edward said. "Pretend I'm Sir John Dalrymple. I've just asked you to dance. What are you going to say?"

"No?"

Edward shook his head. "I'm not even going to hear you, much less believe you, if you say it that way. Try again. I'm Sir John Dalrymple." He bowed from the waist and offered me his hand. "Miss Darcy, would you care to dance?"

I put my head on one side, pretending to consider. "I would love to, Sir John. But I should hate for you to miss the very extensive supper just being laid out in the supper room. I understand from our housekeeper that there are not nearly enough quail's eggs to go around, and only those who come first to the table will be served."

Edward laughed at that and tugged on a stray curl of my hair loosened by the dancing, and I laughed, as well.

I have known Edward all my life—and I have never been shy with him. It would be almost impossible to be so, I think—he is so relaxed and at ease with himself that he sets everyone else at ease, too.

"All right, smart aleck," he said. "That might do it in Sir John's case, I grant you." Then he sobered, and there was a new, unaccustomed note in his voice when he went on. "But what if some other man asks you?"

"Edward, I—" I hesitated, then asked, "What is all this about?"

Even as I asked, I was bracing myself inwardly, because I half expected Edward to bring up George Wickham—and I would be happy never to hear Wickham's name again. But Edward did not answer at once. He shook his head, then turned slightly to look back inside through the open door at the crowded ballroom.

"I'm going to war, Georgiana. What if . . . if I don't come back? I don't want to have to worry about you."

I felt my heart tighten. I put my hand on Edward's. "Edward, I—"

But Edward shook his head before he could finish, forcing a smile. "Never mind me. Just being maudlin, I suppose. Here, we'll have another lesson so that I can march off knowing I've done my duty as guardian.

Pretend I'm a suitor, bent on making improper advances. What do you do?"

He pulled me close to him, one arm going around my waist, the other sliding upwards to angle my face up towards his. I felt my heart contract again—but for quite another reason this time. I felt as though my skin would burst into flames at the heat of his touch. I tried to say something, but I could not. Edward's breath was a stir of warmth against my cheek.

And then Edward's look changed. He had been laughing, smiling down at me with all his old ease. And then something seemed to shift in his eyes and the smile faded from his face.

Time seemed to slow, almost to drag to a stop. The beat of my own heart in my ears seemed unnaturally loud as Edward stared down at me with the strangest look on his face, almost as though he had never seen me before.

And then he stepped back, away from me, shaking his head as though to clear it and clearing his throat. "Just promise me that you'll take care of yourself, that's all."

My mouth had gone dry, but I managed to swallow. "Me? When *you're* the one going off to fight Napoleon's armies?"

The strange look, whatever it had been, was gone from Edward's face. Or maybe I had only imagined it, imagined that moment of charged stillness between us.

He grinned at me. "I'm an officer. We don't do anything dangerous—just stalk about giving orders and looking important."

I raised my eyebrows. "Oh, is that why they gave you this medal?" I touched the medal on his chest, the one he won at the battle of Vimeiro. "For stalking around and looking important?"

Actually, for all I would have known from Edward, he might have won the medal that way. Edward never speaks of the campaigns he has fought or what he has seen and done at war. I practically had to use thumb-screws to even drag the location of the battle out of him.

And it is only from one of his fellow officers, Captain Peabody, that I know Edward really won the medal for leading the charge up a hill to capture a French cannon position.

Edward was still smiling, but there was an edge of sadness or weariness to the smile, and something about his face, the way he held himself made me feel as though he had abruptly stepped back behind a high wall. On impulse, I put out my hand.

"I'll make you a bargain," I said. "I'll promise not to accept proposals from any unsuitable men—and you promise that you'll come back home alive."

For a moment, Edward's eyes were dark and sober on mine. But then he smiled again and put his hand into mine. "Done."

Thursday 28 April 1814

I have been avoiding writing this. But I suppose as long as I am writing down recollections, I should. Even if I do not wish to so much as think of it again, much less recount it here in print.

But then perhaps that is exactly why I should record it here. I can read it over again the next time I think myself flattered by the attentions of another of Mr. Edge-ware's sort.

When I was fifteen, I nearly eloped with George

Wickham.

There. I have written it. And maybe that was the hardest part, and telling the particulars of what happened will not be quite so bad as I thought? That seems a vain hope, but I suppose I'll have to see as I go on.

George Wickham was the son of my father's steward. He was years older than myself, of course. But I can remember him living here on the estate when I was small. He and Fitzwilliam often played together as boys, and they shared a tutor when they got older. And George was kind to me—in an off-hand sort of way. He was a very handsome boy, with fair hair and blue eyes and a ready laugh.

He fell in with a wild, dissipated crowd when he went away to school. But I knew nothing of that. I knew only that while I was staying at Ramsgate with the companion my brother had hired for me, George Wickham chanced to arrive there, as well. Or rather, it was *not* chance. But I did not know that at the time, either.

He was just as he had been when I was growing up—just as handsome, just as ready to laugh and smile. Only he treated me not as a child but as a woman to be courted and adored. We would walk along the beach— with my companion, Mrs. Younge, following a few paces behind—and he would quote poetry to me. Bits of Shakespeare's sonnets, and Wordsworth. He usually got the Shakespeare wrong, but I was far too happy in his company to care.

Was I in love with him? I do not really know, even now. I *wished* to be in love, I do know that much. He was handsome and charming and looked at me—quiet little Georgiana Darcy—as though I were the most beautiful creature in the world. Just as though we were two characters in a novel or one of the poems he recited to me. And I *liked* him—as I always had when I was a child.

And more than that—

It is hard to explain. But I do hate changes. And at fifteen, growing up and entering the world of balls and courtship and marriage felt to me like the most terrifying round of changes that could be imagined. Being courted by George Wickham felt . . . safe, I suppose. Because he was part of that safe, secure world I had known here at Pemberley when I was small, before my parents died.

But then George asked me to elope with him. To run away and be married without my brother's knowledge or consent. I was so shocked I did not know what to say.

I said before that I hate being shy, sometimes. But it is more than that. If I could change one quality in myself, I would wish that I could stand and fight more easily, rather than wanting to run away and hide every time I am shocked or afraid.

And if I still struggle with it now, I was a hundred times worse at just-turned-fifteen.

While I was standing there, feeling my cheeks flush and trying to find words, George kissed me. Not on the hand or on the cheek as he always had done before, but on the mouth.

And all at once I was not happy or flattered any longer. It was frightening, that kiss. He was not gentle or charming, but rough and hungry.

Do all men kiss so? I haven't exactly a wealth of experience to draw from for comparison, having only been kissed on the forehead by my father and brother.

And then that once under the mistletoe by Edward— Colonel Fitzwilliam. Though that scarcely counts, since

I was only ten years old at the time.

I pulled away from George Wickham, but he only laughed and kissed me again and said I had made him the happiest man alive. And then he told me he would make all the arrangements for our elopement. We could travel to Gretna Green in Scotland and be married by declaration only, which of course is legal in Scotland.

I wanted to say something—anything. But I just stood there. Feeling the words lodged in my throat like sharp edged rocks. And then he left me alone in the sitting room of our lodging-house.

I did manage to speak that night to Mrs. Younge, telling her that I was afraid I could not elope and asking her how I ought to tell George Wickham.

But she only said very severely that I was a lucky girl to have attracted the notice of a fine man like Mr. Wickham, and to have the prospect of being wedded at only fifteen years of age.

I lay awake all that night, thinking of how George Wickham had looked at me, how often he had professed his admiration and love. How he had said our marriage would make him the happiest man alive. And I actually cried at the thought of breaking his heart by telling him I could not marry him after all. But perhaps if he were willing to wait a few years—if he would only speak to my brother Fitzwilliam first—

George had said he loved me, after all. And perhaps I would grow to love him in time, after we were married. Not at Gretna Green, but in a proper ceremony in the chapel at Pemberley. Surely my brother would agree, as he and George Wickham had always been close friends—

I cannot believe I was so foolish and easily gulled looking back on it. But that is what ran through my mind at the time.

And then my brother arrived at Ramsgate, too. And I was so relieved.

I suppose that does not show me in a very favourable light, does it? That I was coward enough to be relieved I would not have to muster the backbone to tell George Wickham that I could not elope with him. But since I am being honest, I felt as though I could draw a full breath for the first time in days, the moment I saw my brother walk through the door.

I told my brother the whole—Wickham's courtship, the plan he had made to elope.

And that was when I learned that George Wickham did not love me—had never loved me. The whole of his courtship was merely a ploy to get at my fortune. He had fallen into very dissolute ways and was heavily in debt, and my brother had refused to help him out of his current difficulties. George Wickham had wanted to elope with me first because he knew my brother would never agree to our marriage—and secondly because marrying me would be the neatest revenge he could achieve against Fitzwilliam.

I suppose I never did love George Wickham—because I found I did not feel any disbelief at all when my brother told me the truth of his character. Maybe a part of me had sensed all along that for all his charm, he was dishonourable at his core.

George left Ramsgate at once. At least I never had to see him again.

Now George Wickham is married to Elizabeth's youngest sister, Lydia. That is almost the only time I have ever seen Elizabeth look truly sad or sorrowful: when she speaks of Lydia's marriage. Though when I told her once that I hated to think of George Wickham taking advantage of her sister's trust, she said a little bitterly that Lydia had known full well what she was about.

No one save for Edward, Fitzwilliam, and Elizabeth knows of what happened at Ramsgate between George Wickham and me. Besides Wickham and myself, I mean.

No one can know. My reputation would be irretrievably lost if it ever were known that I had been on the brink of such an elopement—that I had been unchaperoned in George Wickham's company, besides.

Which may be utterly unjust, but it is the way of the world.

I do not think I ever did truly love George Wickham—and if I was infatuated, a little, I told Elizabeth the truth when I said that was long gone, now. It is just that recounting the whole of the hateful episode here has made me feel—

But I am going to stop feeling sorry for myself. I would be happy to stay here at Pemberley—what I said to Elizabeth on that score was true, as well. I am happy here, even if I never find a suitor who actually wishes to marry me, instead of my thirty thousand pounds.

The rain is streaming down outside the windows and has been since last night; I could hear it drumming on the roof as I lay in bed. Now my brother is busy with his accounts and the running of the estate in his study. The other men of the house party are playing at billiards in the game room, and I am with the ladies in the drawing room, sitting in my favourite place at the window seat. Caroline is looking at a book on the settee—flipping through the pages and looking sulky because the men have abandoned us today and it's too wet outside to ask any of them to go outside and walk in the grounds.

Elizabeth is sewing, and my Aunt de Bourgh is sitting next to her making observations like, "What a pity you cannot sew as well as I could in my youth. You would need a magnifying glass to see the stitch work in the sampler I made at school."

Elizabeth has just smiled and said, very politely, "Thank you so much for telling me. I must be sure to have a magnifying glass on hand if you should ever choose to show it to me. I should hate not to be able to appreciate it in full."

My aunt is sitting and frowning and trying to work out whether she has been insulted or not.

And the papers today say there are to be great balls in London to celebrate the Marquess of Wellington's victory over Napoleon.

Friday 29 April 1814

Edward is engaged.

Maybe I should write that a hundred times in a copy book, the way our schoolmistresses used to make naughty pupils copy out their faults when I was at school.

Edward is engaged. Edward is engaged. Edward is—

No, actually I do not need to write it out. That is just the trouble: I am convinced enough of it already. The knowledge of it is like a black beetle in a cup of tea, completely spoiling my memory of today.

(*What an elegant analogy, Georgiana*, I can hear my aunt saying in tones of deepest sarcasm if she were ever to read this diary. Which of course, she never will. I either carry it in my reticule or hide it in my room under the mattress on my bed, where even my Aunt de Bourgh would never bother to look.)

The trouble is that I do not care whether he is engaged or not to Miss Mary Graves. Or rather, *I* may care, but my heart apparently does not. If I were being melodramatic, I would say that my heart is at this moment aching far more than my sprained ankle, which is currently wrapped up in bandages and propped on a stool in front of me.

At least my hair has finally dried.

But I had better write it all down properly.

Edward arrived today, fully four days before we expected him. He had stayed the night in Nottingham to rest and stable his horse, and then rode out for Pemberley at first light this morning. Though since he had sent no word, we of course had no idea he was coming.

I had slipped out for a walk, because I had overheard my aunt speaking to Mr. Folliet and telling him how much she knew I wanted him to accompany me on a ride. In company with Dawson and two of her menservants, of course. My aunt would never suggest anything so improper as my riding out alone in company with a man.

I have scarcely spoken to Mr. Folliet, but he seems perfectly amiable. And not at all vain, despite looking so much like Sir Lancelot. But standing there beside the French doors in the morning room and hearing my aunt speak to him, I found myself imagining exactly what the proposed ride would be like: me feeling as though I ought to be making polite conversation with Mr. Folliet, but having no idea what to say. He either bored to tears or trying to ingratiate himself.

The two serving men looking on and probably laughing silently. Poor, long-suffering Dawson taking note of every word said so that she could report it to my aunt. Not that I blame her for it. If I were my Aunt de Bourgh's maidservant, I would probably spy for my aunt, too, just to keep the peace.

But still, I suddenly felt I absolutely could not do it, could not go riding or be pushed into an acquaintance with Mr. Folliet that—unless he is in more dire financial straits than my aunt thinks—he probably wishes for no more than I do. So I slipped out the French doors and into the garden and went for a walk.

Which was very childish and cowardly, and I was properly punished for it, because I had come out without a bonnet or a pelisse, only my shawl, and the morning air was quite chilly. And even worse, I was wearing thin slippers instead of boots, and the ground was very muddy with all the recent rain. By the time I had gone a hundred yards, my shoes were more black than pink. But even so, I kept going. And not just because I didn't want to go back to the house and face my aunt.

The air was clear and the sun was gloriously bright, and the grounds of the park felt fairly bursting with the promise of spring: all the new leaves and buds on the trees, the shoots of daffodils just poking up from the soil.

Without thinking, I had taken the usual path, through the woods and across the stream. I had just crossed the bridge when my already mud-slick slippers slid on a fresh patch of mud. I lost my footing, tried to catch hold of the bridge railing, but my hand only slipped off that as well, and before I knew it, I had tumbled the whole way down the embankment and landed with a splash in the stream itself.

The cold water was like a slap in the face, and I'd had the breath completely knocked out of me. But when I tried to push myself up, I found I could, so I knew I was not really hurt. My heart was still hammering, though, and I was struggling to catch my breath, so that I had only managed to pull myself into a sitting position when all of a sudden strong arms were lifting me up, clear of the water.

That made my heart jump again, but then I recognised the voice that spoke in my ear. "Georgiana! Good God, are you hurt?"

I pushed the wet hair out of my face and looked up, and sure enough it was Edward who was holding me, one arm about my shoulders, the other under my knees so that he could carry me up the bank.

He wore his red army coat, and his hair was a little longer than I remembered. And there was a thin white line—a new scar—running down one of his lean brown cheeks.

I tried to speak but was still too much out of breath, so I could only nod.

"I was riding through the park, and saw you fall," Edward said. I was still pressed up against him. I could feel how hard his heart was hammering in his chest. "What on earth are you doing out here all on your own?"

"Just walking," I managed to say.

The tight line of Edward's mouth relaxed at that. "Well, next time try to include fewer dives into freezing cold stream beds on your walks. Less dramatic, but far more comfortable."

I would have said something indignant to that, but the stream *had* been freezing cold and I was drenched to the skin; even the shawl I'd had wrapped around my shoulders was soaked. I had started to shiver and my teeth were chattering so much I couldn't make myself form the words.

Edward set me down on a dry, grassy patch beside the path and knelt beside me, shrugging out of his army coat. "Here—take this." He wrapped it around my shoulders. "It will be yards too big on you, but at least it's dry."

"Th-thank you," I managed to say.

The first time I see Edward in nearly a year, and I had managed to go tumbling into a stream like a clumsy six-year-old. And now I was covered in mud and looking like a drowned rat.

Fate really does have a very peculiar sense of humour at times.

And then I saw it: a stain, bright scarlet and wet on the shoulder of Edward's white linen shirt.

"You're hurt—you're bleeding!" I said. His lifting me up the embankment must have re-opened the wound in his shoulder.

I sat up. "Take off your shirt."

Edward's eyebrows shot up. "What—here?"

"It's better than bleeding to death!"

Edward glanced down at his own shoulder for the first time. The stain was at least the size of my hand, and spreading, but he shrugged and said, "It's nothing much. I'll have it seen to when we get to the house."

"We're three miles from the house at least," I said. My teeth were still chattering, but the warmth of his coat was helping and I didn't feel nearly so cold. "Let me at least bind it up for you before it gets any worse."

Edward's jaw clamped shut. "I thought young ladies were supposed to faint at the sight of blood."

"And I thought soldiers were supposed to know how to keep themselves alive!"

Edward's mouth twitched again at that. He looked at me, then shook his head, and finally undid the ties on his shirt and slid it off one shoulder. "All right, if it will satisfy you. But it's really not serious."

The wound had been bound up with a thick linen pad, but the bandage was entirely saturated with blood. I untied the bindings, and Edward drew in breath through his teeth when I peeled the final layers back; they'd been stuck to his skin with dried blood.

I did feel a bit queasy at the sight of the bloody furrow in the muscle of his upper arm. I suppose the injury must be two or three weeks old by now, but it still looked ugly, angry and red and puckered around the edges.

"You should have a physician look at this," I said. "It doesn't look as though it's healing properly to me."

Edward looked down at me, eyebrows raised again. "You mean to tell me you don't number doctoring among your varied accomplishments?"

I realised abruptly that I was sitting nearly in Edward's lap, my drenched clothes plastered to me, and with one hand braced against his bare chest. I felt my cheeks start to heat up, even as the contact with Edward's skin seemed to jolt through my every nerve.

"Do you have a handkerchief?" I asked, as matter-of-factly as I could. Because it was bad enough to have been pulled like a drowned kitten from the stream. It would be worse yet to start blushing and stammering like some silly schoolgirl.

"What?"

"Your handkerchief—give it to me. Unless you've clean bandages about you. But I need something to pad the wound."

I did manage to make a fresh pad for the wound from my handkerchief and his. Even if I could not stop my pulse from racing every time I had to touch him.

When I had finished, Edward unclamped his teeth. "Now will you let me get you back to the house?" He started to lift me again, but I shook my head. "I'm all right, now. I can walk."

But when I tried to stand, my ankle gave a sharp, sudden throb and buckled under me. I had not felt it before, but I suppose I must have twisted it when I fell. I would have fallen again if Edward had not been so quick to catch me.

He is very strong; I could feel the hard muscles of his arms even through the layers of his coat. And before I could argue or pull away, he turned his head—he still had his good arm around me, supporting my weight—and whistled softly, two short trills and one long. A chestnut horse stepped out of the shade of the trees and onto the path, and Edward said, "This is King. He'll carry you with even less trouble than I could."

We neither of us spoke on the ride back to the house, and when we drew close to the front steps Edward pulled up on the reins to stop the horse, then simply sat there, staring at the front door.

I suppose now that the immediate crisis was past, we neither of us knew quite what to say. In the space of half an hour, I had been dunked in the stream, pulled out by Edward, then demanded his handkerchief to bandage a bullet wound.

Finally Edward swung himself down out of the saddle and reached up to help me down, as well. "So, Georgiana," he said. "How have you been these last months?"

I couldn't help it: I started to laugh, and Edward joined me, laughing so hard that we were both entirely out of breath. And then, all at once he stopped and just stood there, looking down at me.

He still had his arms round me from helping me off the horse, and we were so close that I could see the tiny flecks of gold in his brown eyes, the tiny laugh lines at the corners of his mouth. I could feel the steady beating of his heart, the warmth of his body seeping into mine.

I stopped shivering, stopped laughing, stopped even breathing. I felt as though I were a dragonfly in amber, trapped by the weight of his gaze.

And then the front door opened, and Elizabeth came running down the steps. "Georgiana, there you are! And Edward! But"—she looked from one of us to the other, taking in my soaking wet dress and Edward's bloodied shoulder. "But what's happened to you? Are you all right?"

Edward let go of me so fast I nearly fell over. He did put a hand under my elbow to steady me, but he did not look at me again as he said to Elizabeth, "She's all right, just a slight fall into the stream. Though you may want to summon the local physician to look at that ankle."

Then he tipped his hat and strode past Elizabeth into the house without once looking round.

Elizabeth wanted to summon two of the footmen to help carry me into the house, but I would not let her. My ankle was not nearly so painful as it had been. And besides, I had more than reached my limit on the number of people I wanted to see me in my drowned-rat state.

With Elizabeth's help, I hobbled up to my room, and Elizabeth called for the servants to bring kettles for a hot bath. She stayed to help me wash the mud out of my hair. But she didn't ask me to talk—which I was very, very grateful for—only helped me to dress and then wrap up my ankle. She asked if I wanted the physician, but I said I didn't. It's only a slight sprain, and he could do nothing but tell me what I already know, that it will be painful for a day or two, then gradually less so.

Elizabeth said I ought to rest and left me to sleep

if I could. But I can not, so I have taken up this book instead.

Would it be terribly cowardly to pretend I've taken a chill? Or say that my ankle is far too painful for me to go down to dinner tonight?

I am afraid it would. Besides, I can hardly stay in my room the entire month Edward is here. I will have to face him again sometime.

What did he see in that frozen moment when he looked down into my eyes? I wasn't thinking of trying to guard my feelings—I wasn't thinking of anything. So he very likely saw little Georgiana Darcy, who he suddenly realised has a schoolgirl's infatuation with him.

That is probably why he left so abruptly—he realised how awkward it was going to be. My father's will left him my co-guardian, along with my brother. And now his fond little charge fancies herself in love with him.

He is probably even now trying to decide how to let me down gently and inform me of his engagement to Miss Graves in the kindest possible way. Because he is fond of me. Of course he wouldn't want to hurt my feelings.

I've just realised that I am grinding my teeth together so hard my jaw is aching. I have to stop. I have to stop and think how I am going to act the next time I see Edward. I will have to be very polite and very cool and collected and calm. And it would help if I could convince him that he was entirely mistaken, and that I'm actually in love with someone else.

Maybe I can persuade myself to develop a violent passion for Sir John's greasy hair and gooseberry eyes and endless talk of guns.

For one thing, I don't want Edward feeling sorry for

me.

But for another, if he truly is happy in his engagement to Miss Graves, I don't want that shadowed by worry for me. Edward deserves better than that.

Saturday 30 April 1814

I did go down to dinner last night. I did not manage to fall violently in love with Sir John. But I did speak to Mr. Folliet for some time. He is very nice. Really, as nice as he is handsome.

Elizabeth said she was feeling a little indisposed after dinner and went to lie down in her room, and my brother went with her, to be sure she was not seriously ill. Sir John proposed a game of whist, and my Aunt de Bourgh allowed herself to be persuaded, though she did decree that Anne was feeling tired and sent her off to bed first.

Mr. Folliet came over to sit beside me, where I was perched in my usual place on the window seat, reading.

"I feel I ought to apologise, Miss Darcy." He has a voice that exactly matches his face: deep-pitched and very attractive.

"Apologise? Why?"

"Because any girl who is so horrified by the prospect of going riding with me that she hurls herself into icy cold rivers to avoid it must clearly dislike me a good deal. Therefore, I must have done something to offend, and should apologise." He smiled. "Though my apology would be a good deal more convincing if you told me what it is I've done."

I could feel colour flaming in my cheeks. Of course the entire house party knew about my misadventure. I would have been perfectly happy to have no one but Edward and Elizabeth hear that I had tumbled into the stream. But of course I had to give some explanation for why I was limping and needed Elizabeth's help in managing the stairs.

"Tell me," Mr. Folliet was saying, "and I'll apologise in earnest and we can begin again. I promise I'm not so terrible once you get to know me. You've only got one other ankle, and it would be a shame to sprain that one, too, by throwing yourself into another river the next time your aunt decides that you're longing to show me Pemberley's grounds on horseback."

I set down my book and looked up at him. My cheeks were still burning. But in a way it was freeing to be able to speak openly, because I surely could not become any more embarrassed than I already was.

"I'm sorry, Mr. Folliet. It's surely not escaped your notice that my Aunt de Bourgh is intent on hurling me at the heads of any and every eligible young man under Pemberley's roof."

"Lady Catherine is certainly a force to be reckoned with," Mr. Folliet agreed.

"But there's no reason you should suffer for it. You should feel free to invent your own excuses the next time she tries to force us together. I won't hold it against you, I promise."

"What about what you want?" Mr. Folliet asked.

"Do you mean, do I want to be paraded in front of my aunt's collection of suitors like a prize-winning horse at a show?" I felt my mouth twist. "Not especially, no."

Mr. Folliet was watching me. "And what about your brother? Couldn't he speak to your aunt on your behalf?"

"He would—if I asked him to. He's one of the very few people in the world who *does* stand up to my aunt— and whom she actually accepts that she can't bully."

"But you haven't spoken to him?"

I shook my head. Because it's not only that I'm not accustomed to sharing such confidences with my brother. "It seems so childish, calling on my elder brother to speak for me to my own aunt," I finally said. "I ought to be able to stand up to her, as well. It's not as though she can actually do anything but be unpleasant if I tell her I don't want to marry any of the men she's chosen for me. It's just—"

It's just that I hate unpleasantness, and loud voices and yelling. And just the thought of the scene my Aunt de Bourgh would create if I ever did speak out so made my stomach lurch and all my nerves clench. But I recollected myself, and recalled that Mr. Folliet was almost a complete stranger. "I'm sorry—we needn't go on speaking of this. You must think me childish indeed."

Mr. Folliet looked away for a moment, towards the card table where my aunt was sitting between Edward and Sir John. "I think . . . I think that it's not always easy to be honest, and especially with family members." His voice had a note of something, something lonely or sad that I didn't understand. But then he shook his head as though to clear it and smiled again. "Well, then. I'll just have to tell your aunt that you've broken my heart and turned me down—and do something so spectacularly unsuitable that she finds your refusal utterly justified. Would it help if I stood under your window at night, looking mournful and reciting bad poetry? Or playing a guitar? I don't actually know how to play the guitar, but I suppose I could learn."

I laughed. "Please don't do anything so drastic on my account."

I felt my aunt look up at us when I laughed. Likely she was congratulating herself on the success of her matchmaking scheme.

I think out of the corner of my eye, I saw Edward watching us, too, but I would not let myself look at him.

Before we parted for the night, Mr. Folliet asked me to go riding with him tomorrow after church. I said I would be delighted.

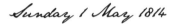

Tonight I happened to be passing my brother's study on my way upstairs to bed, and I saw Fitzwilliam and Elizabeth together inside. I did not mean to spy, but the door was partway open, and as I walked past I saw Elizabeth curled up on the floor in front of the fire, leaning her shoulder up against my brother's chair. She was wearing the short-sleeved green satin gown she'd had on at dinner, and the firelight ran golden along her face and bare arms, and twined golden highlights in her hair.

She said something—I didn't hear what—and tilted her head back to smile up at him.

And Fitzwilliam said something low and husky and leaned down to kiss her on the mouth.

I walked away quickly—and neither of them saw me. But I can still feel a little lonely, hollow ache inside my chest.

It's not that I am envious. Well, I suppose if I'm being completely truthful, I do envy them a bit. More than a bit. Or rather, not them so much as what they have found in each other.

I couldn't love either Elizabeth or my brother more. And I want them to be happy, truly. I'm so glad that they are.

But—

Never mind. I'm even going to irritate myself if I keep going on in this vein.

Let me think what else I can write about.

I learned several new measures of a Mozart sonata on the pianoforte today. I finally had the chance to practice alone, since I came downstairs in the morning more than an hour earlier than anyone else.

And I did go riding with Mr. Folliet. A small part of me wishes I could report that I do not like him, just because my aunt is so determined that I shall. But I do like him, actually. He's very charming and agreeable—and doesn't seem at all vain of his good looks. He is very easy to talk to, as well. I did not feel at all shy.

A larger part of me wishes that my heart raced and my skin tingled when Mr. Folliet speaks to me or touches my hand. But it has not happened yet.

Monday 2 May 1814

I have not seen Edward at all today.

Which I will admit is more than partly by design, since I stayed upstairs in my room this morning until I saw my brother and Edward riding out away from the house.

Mrs. Reynolds came to speak to me about him, though, almost as soon as I came downstairs.

Mrs. Reynolds is our housekeeper—and has been since years before I was born. She is plump and red-faced and very fierce in her manner—all the kitchen staff and the maids are terrified of her. She bullies both Edward and my brother unmercifully because she has known them both since they were small boys and Edward used to come and spend his summers here.

This morning her face was anxious, though, as she

stopped me in the front hall. "It's Mr. Edward," she said, when I'd asked whether anything was wrong. "He doesn't seem a bit like himself."

Against my will, I felt my heart contract. It would be so much easier if I could just order myself to stop caring so much about him.

"Maybe his shoulder is paining him," I said. "We should make sure he sees the physician."

"Aye, I've sent for him," Mrs. Reynolds said. "He'll be here this afternoon. But there's more than that ailing Mr. Edward, I'd say. He's so thin and brown—and he scarcely touched a bite of supper last night. And there's more. I gave him his old room—the one he always slept in when he came to stay here as a boy."

I nodded.

"Well," Mrs. Reynolds said, "This morning, Mr. Edward comes to me and says he doesn't want that room— he'd rather have one in the east wing. The east wing! I ask you. Where most of the rooms aren't even in use, and half the chimneys won't draw on account of it's been so long since a fire was lighted in them."

"What did you tell him?" I asked.

"What could I tell him?" Mrs. Reynolds spread her hands. "I told him I'd find him a room in the east wing. He's a grown man, I reckon he can sleep where he likes. It just seems strange to me, that's all."

I thought of the wound in his shoulder, the new scar on his cheek. "He's just come back from war," I said. "Perhaps he just needs space—time to himself to adjust. And he's ridden out with my brother this morning. Maybe he'll speak to Fitzwilliam if there's something really wrong."

"Aye. Maybe." Mrs. Reynolds nodded her head, though she did not look convinced.

I'm not sure I am, either. But neither do I think there is anything else I can do. Not because I am resolved not to throw myself at Edward—because I would risk humiliation, if I thought I could help him.

It sounds a strange thing to say about anyone so relaxed and amiable as he is, but Edward is a private person, in many ways. He does not share his innermost thoughts easily.

Unless and until he decides to speak to one of us, I do not think anyone will find out if there really is anything wrong.

Tuesday 3 May 1814

From the time I was twelve, any time Edward would go off to fight abroad, I would sit down at the pianoforte and play *Robin Adair* whenever I was afraid for him.

Maybe that is a strange choice, since *Robin Adair* is such a sad song. And maybe it was; to be honest, at first I only played it because I was twelve years old and it was almost the only song I could play without any mistakes. But then after a while . . . I don't know. Somehow I would play it, and it would always make me feel better. As though my worrying and missing him had been poured into the song and so lifted out of me.

That sounds as though I am one of those romantic, sentimental girls who wander about out-of-doors quoting Wordsworth's poems in the middle of thunderstorms. I'm not sure how to put it so that it does not sound overly romantical and silly, though.

It's just that that is what music has always done for me, ever since I was quite small: given me a place to put the feelings that hurt most.

I was in the music room this morning, practising the

Mozart sonata again. But I could not seem to keep my mind on the musical score in front of me. I kept getting my fingering wrong and losing the tempo—and finally I gave up and let my hands travel, just idly, over the keys.

I had not really meant to play anything in particular, but almost before I realised it, my fingers had fallen into the tune of Robin Adair. I started to sing, as well—just softly.

What's this dull town to me
  Robin's not near
What was't I wish'd to see
  What wish'd to hear
Where all the joy and mirth
  Made this town heaven on earth
Oh, they're all fled with thee
  Robin Adair

I played it all through, and then a slight sound behind me made me turn on the pianoforte bench. Edward was standing just inside the doorway. He must have been listening to me play for some time, because he was standing quite still, leaning up against the doorframe, with his arms folded across his chest.

My heart stumbled and quickened in my chest, and I must have gasped because Edward smiled a little and said, "I'm sorry, I didn't mean to frighten you. It's just I didn't want to interrupt you. And it's a long time since I've heard you play."

He was wearing civilian clothes today rather than his army uniform: tan breeches and boots and a maroon coat. His right arm was in a sling.

I know I resolved before to be distant and calm and cool the next time I was with Edward. But sitting there, in the same room with him, I could feel all that resolve slipping away. The war is over—and he has returned alive.

And he is a friend, even if he will never be anything more.

"How is your shoulder?" I asked.

"It's fine. A little sore, that's all. I could leave off the sling—but Mr. Broyles threatened me with dire consequences if I didn't wear it for a day or two."

"Old Mr. Broyles or young?" I asked.

"There are two of them?"

"Father and son," I said. "Both physicians in Lambton; they have a practice together. Though it must have been the father you saw—I can't imagine your having been intimidated into wearing a sling by the son. He's a very nice young man, but not terribly imposing."

"Wait a moment," Edward said. "Thin? Spectacles? Ears like flying gibbets?"

"Flying gibbets is a little unkind. But they do stick out, I grant you. And yes, that's young Mr. Broyles."

Edward nodded. "He came to call along with his father, but I took him for an assistant." He raised his eyebrows at me, "And come to think of it, he asked after you—and said to give you his compliments. Do I need to go charging down to their offices in Lambton and defend your honour?"

"From young Mr. Broyles? Good heavens, no, you'd scare him to death. Besides, he's already engaged to the daughter of a local landowner. He came to the house last year when half of the servants were ill with influenza, that's all—and I helped him with doses and heating water and all the rest because half the servants *were* ill and there wasn't anyone else."

Edward wiped his brow theatrically. "Well, that's all right then. I was afraid I was going to have to play the stern, heavy-handed guardian and lock you in your room."

I laughed. "Heavy-handed guardian? When you're

only ten years older than I am?"

"Ten years?" Edward turned away to look out the window as something crossed his face like a swift shadow. "At the moment it feels as if I'm a great deal older than that."

I looked at him. I know his face almost as well as I do my own, and today in the morning light filtering through the windows he looked thinner than when last I had seen him. He's sun-browned from living on campaign, with fine lines about the corners of his eyes.

Edward has always been of an open disposition, relaxed and easy in company and very self-assured. He and Elizabeth do have similar temperaments in that way, even if he was never really in love with her. Just like Elizabeth, Edward jokes and teases a good deal, and can laugh and banter with very nearly anyone.

He had been speaking in almost his usual way. But as he spoke the final words, there was a new note in his voice. And there was just at that moment a hint of . . . I'm not quite sure. Darkness or sadness or something about the look in his eyes.

"How are you, Edward? I mean, how are you really?" I asked him.

Edward lifted one shoulder. His eyes were still fixed out the window. "It turned out there was a fragment of the musket ball still lodged in the wound that was keeping it from healing properly. Broyles the elder dug it out for me and gave me something he said would help draw any further impurities out."

"I'm glad," I said. "But that wasn't what I meant."

It is true, what I wrote yesterday, about thinking there little point in questioning Edward unless he was ready to talk.

But there was something that looked almost . . . almost lost about him as he stood, staring out the window.

"Mrs. Reynolds told me you asked to change your room," I said, after a moment's hesitation.

Edward was silent. Then his shoulders moved again. "I didn't . . . I don't fit into the old room anymore."

I waited, but he did not say anything more, only stood at the window with his shoulders tensed. "It must seem very strange to be back here, at Pemberley," I finally said.

This time, the silence lasted so long I thought Edward wasn't going to speak at all. But then he said, "It is . . . strange. I suppose that's as good a word as any." Edward rubbed the space between his eyes. "Strange to eat off china plates instead of my tin mess kit. Strange to suddenly sleep in a real bed again instead of on a camp cot or more often muddy ground." He turned and gave me a brief flash of almost his usual smile. "The first night after I landed in England—I was staying at an inn—and I had to pull the blankets off the bed and lie down on the floor before I could get off to sleep. The chamber maid tripped over me in the morning when she came in to lay the fire—she must have thought I was out of my senses."

Then his smile faded. He looked out the window again, resting one hand against the pane of glass, his eyes travelling over the view of the lawns, dotted with Spanish oaks and elms. The lake in front of the house, and the woods beyond.

"It's an odd feeling, too, to come back here and find all this"—he spread one hand to indicate the view—"so much unchanged. Everything looks as it always has. Completely untouched by anything that's happened in the outside world."

Edward shook his head as though to clear it, then seemed to force a smile. "Strange—but good, too, I suppose, to find it so. It makes me feel as though Pemberley is a small, bespelled pocket that the caprices of time and chance can never touch."

I moved to stand next to him at the window. "I know—I've always loved that feeling about it, too," I said.

Edward turned. He didn't speak, though, just looked down into my eyes. And there it was again—just for that instant, the dark, shadowed look was there at the back of his gaze.

And then the door opened behind us and he instantly stepped back, away from me.

It was Elizabeth—come, she said, to summon us both to breakfast.

"Mrs. Reynolds says you've come back from the war all bones and need to be fattened," she said to Edward, smiling. "If you don't take a good enough breakfast, I think she has every intention of picking up a spoon and feeding you herself."

Edward laughed. "I may have faced down Napoleon's armies, but I know better than to cross Mrs. Reynolds when her mind is made up. All right, I'll come."

He spoke so easily and his smile was so carefree that I could almost believe I had imagined that lost look in his eyes.

Wednesday 4 May 1814

My mother died when I was six years old. I am glad we have the portrait in the upstairs gallery that my father had painted of her, because it helps me to remember her now. It hurts that my true memories of her are so much faded—but they are. And looking up at the portrait helps bring remembrance back, at least a little.

She was beautiful. I wish I looked like her, but I don't, not at all. She was fine-boned and small, with golden hair, blue eyes and a heart-shaped face.

She used to sew little dolls for me when I was very small—a whole collection of them. I have them, still, in a drawer in my room. Milk maids and tiny swaddled babies and fine ladies dressed in scraps cut from the remnants of her worn-out gowns. She made a doll-sized version of our family for me, too: a little doll of my father, dressed in his breeches and his green riding coat; one of my brother, as he was at twelve or thirteen, very tall and thin and with a mop of unruly black hair; and doll versions of herself and me, wearing matching white dresses and blue sashes.

She used to take me out into the garden with her, too, and we would read from storybooks or play at skittles and spillikins.

My father would laugh when he found us together, my mother with her hair coming down and her skirts spotted with dirt and bits of grass. And my mother would laugh, too, and say she never could learn to behave as a fine lady ought.

My father's heart was broken when she died. He did try his best to comfort me—but he had his own grief to think of, and my brother's, as well as mine. And all the relations who had come to stay for her funeral. And I didn't want to see anyone—not my father, nor Fitzwilliam nor anyone else. I think I spent the entire week after the funeral hiding under furniture—tables and sofas and chairs. Hoping no one would see me, and I would not be forced to come out and speak to anyone.

That was how I came to overhear two of my older girl cousins, who were sitting together in the library: I had crept under the library table and fallen asleep, and woke up to find them sitting on the sofa just inches away from me. So I stayed frozen where I was, not daring to move.

They were speaking of the novel they had been reading—a grisly story about an abbey inhabited by the ghost of a drowned monk that haunted any visitor who dared spend a night under the abbey's roof. I had never heard anything like it before. And at six, I didn't understand that it was only a story; I believed every word.

And after that I couldn't go to sleep at night. I was terrified that the moment I closed my eyes, I'd see my sweet, happy, lovely mother, come back to haunt us all as a horrible ghost.

It was Edward who found me sobbing under the table in the dining room late one night. My nurse was supposed to sleep with me in the outer room of the nursery, of course. But I had waited until I heard her snoring and then crept past her, because I could not bear to lie there in bed any more, waiting for my mother's ghost to appear.

Edward was sixteen and had just received his first army commission. He picked me up and found some wine that had been left on the sideboard and poured me a glass. He watered it down so much that it was almost all water and scarcely any wine, but I didn't know that and thought it was very grown-up. I had never tasted wine before.

Then, while I was drinking it, he finally got me to tell him what had frightened me. And then the next day he got a whole box of the most gothic, grisly books he could find from the lending library—full of haunted castles and skeletons and swooning heroines—and sat next to my little bed in the nursery and read them to me every night.

Which sounds like a very strange sort of cure. But he made the stories incredibly comical—exaggerating all the horrible groans and gasps, clutching his forehead at the stupidity of the heroines, who *would* persist in going into the forbidden wings of the castle all alone, and at night.

I would sit there with him, giggling while he read. And then afterwards I would be able to go to sleep.

Edward stayed for a full three weeks, which was a longer leave of absence than he'd been granted by his Colonel. I found out afterwards that he would have been disciplined except that the peace treaty—the first peace treaty—with Napoleon had just been signed and everyone in the army was in a celebratory mood.

I remember watching him ride away at the end of his stay and trying to decide just how old I would have to be before I could marry him. I think I decided on twelve— at twelve, I thought, I would surely be old enough.

My fingers are itching to draw Edward now. But I'll draw Mr. Folliet instead.

Thursday 5 May 1814

I have actually had a real conversation with my cousin Anne. Not a long talk, true, but at least we did not speak only about her headaches or weak eyes— at least not entirely. Though I still cannot say it went especially well, or ended with any appreciable progress towards my knowing her better or helping her in any way.

Well, I may have stopped her throwing herself out of a second story window. I suppose that must be counted as progress.

I have been thinking about her since I was watching her the other night, after supper. She was sitting in her usual place by the fire, but instead of huddling under her lap rugs and simply staring at the floor as she usually does, she was watching Caroline and Mr. Carter, my brother's clergyman friend. Caroline and Mr. Carter were speaking together. Or rather, Caroline was speaking and Mr. Carter was blushing and stammering whenever he was addressed.

But he seemed far from unhappy for all that—and he did look at Caroline as though he admired her.

My cousin Anne was watching them both, and just for a moment I caught a flash of such naked misery on her face that my own heart constricted as though a giant hand had wrapped around my ribs and squeezed.

No one should be that unhappy. Or go through her life without ever actually doing any living of it.

I wished—I still wish—that I could help her somehow. And today there seemed to be a chance, because we've been invited to a dinner party tomorrow by Mr. and Mrs. Herron, an older couple who live on the estate neighbouring ours.

My Aunt de Bourgh has taken a chill—a true chill, for she was coughing and shivering last night at dinner. She has sent for the physician, who has told her to stay in bed for the next three days at least. So of course my aunt has said she would not be going along to the party.

Which I can understand, for she really is ill. But then she decreed that my cousin Anne would, by tomorrow, have taken a chill as well. And so Anne would not be able to go to dinner at the Herrons', either.

I should like to know how, exactly, my aunt imagines Anne would ever manage to take a chill, when she does nothing but sit by the fire in the warmest rooms of the house, absolutely smothered in shawls and lap rugs. She never goes outside if there's so much as a hint of rain, and she never even walks through dewy grass for fear of getting her feet wet. If she or my aunt could manage a way that she could avoid getting wet even in the bath, I imagine they would immediately put it into practice.

But I could not stop remembering how miserable she looked the other night. So this morning after breakfast I went along to her room to see if I could not persuade her into going to the dinner party tomorrow night after all.

Her door was closed, so I tapped on the panel. But the latch had not quite shut, so when I knocked, the door popped open, and I saw my cousin Anne, kneeling on the bedroom window ledge with the window wide open, her arms outspread and her head thrown back.

"Anne!" I cried out.

Likely it was not the wisest thing to do, calling out and risking startling her while she was perched so precariously like that. But her head jerked round at the sound of my voice, and she fell inside the room instead of out the window.

I let out a breath of relief. "What on earth were you doing up there?"

Anne scrambled up from the carpet where she had landed. The fresh air had whipped some colour into her sallow cheeks. But the moment her eyes met mine, the usual sullen, discontented look slid back over her face.

She shrugged and turned to pull the window closed. "Nothing."

Her voice was so flat and expressionless I felt the back of my neck prickle with cold. "You must have been doing *something*, climbing up onto the window ledge like that."

Anne pulled a shawl—a brown, hideously ugly woollen one—round her shoulders, and would not meet my eyes. "I have a headache. I thought some fresh air might help." She looked up at me then. "What do you want, Georgiana? I'm not feeling very well this morning. No, don't sit down." I'd made a slight movement towards one of the chairs. "I would prefer you didn't stay. It will make my head ache to talk to you."

I looked at her and wondered if this was what happened when you spent a lifetime under my aunt's thumb, being ordered around as though you were five years old. You never got the chance to stop *behaving* as though you were five.

That was what Anne reminded me of: a sulky, spoiled five-year-old, too occupied with herself to even think of good manners.

"I wanted to ask if you'd consider coming to the party tomorrow after all," I said. "I know your mother said you'd have a chill—but you haven't have you? You could ride in the carriage with Elizabeth and Caroline and me. My brother will be on horseback, and I imagine the rest of the men will, too. There'll be plenty of room."

Anne stared at me. Then she narrowed her eyes. "Why?" she asked. "Why should you want me to come? No one ever wants me to come anywhere with them."

She said it in the same discontented voice as before. But it struck me all of a sudden that it's entirely true. In Anne's entire life, I doubt anyone has ever actually wanted her to be anywhere. Except maybe her mother wanting her to sit by the fire and stay in bed.

Anne was still watching me. "Admit it," she said, almost as though she'd heard my thought. "There's not one single person under the roof of Pemberley House who would actually want to be in my company for more than five minutes."

"Mr. Carter seemed to enjoy speaking with you very much, the evening he first arrived," I protested. "What were you talking of?"

"We were speaking of China," Anne said.

"China?" I could scarcely have been more surprised if Anne had said they'd been discussing the feeding habits of sea slugs. To be honest, I would not have even thought that Anne knew where China was.

But a touch of colour warmed her cheeks. "Oh, yes! I've read all about it. I love travel books. All about China and Egypt and the Amazon. I don't get to read them often—my mother thinks they strain my eyes, so I have to find ways to look at them in secret. But I'd read the one Mr. Carter happened to have taken down from your brother's shelves, and we were talking about that. Did you know, Georgiana, that there's a Forbidden City in China? A whole city where only the Emperor and the members of his court can walk. And the streets are paved with gold bricks, so they say. The author of the book had never been there himself. Only heard rumours, you know."

"I didn't know that," I said. Maybe I shouldn't have said anything at all—or maybe it was inevitable, but the instant I spoke, the spell was broken. All the animation went out of Anne's face, like a candle flame blown out by a gust of wind.

She turned her head away. "It doesn't matter. Mr. Carter only spoke to me that night because he didn't know who I was. He hadn't yet become acquainted with me and realised what a gloomy, dismal invalid I am."

I did not say that she could try changing her temperament if she wanted people to like her. Anne was not in a mood to listen. And besides, even I know that it is not so easy as that.

I remember one of the girls at school telling me I should just stop being so shy. I was not really friends with her, but I liked her well enough—and still, just for a second after she said it, I could have hit her with something.

"I would like you to come," I said to Anne. I made my voice as warm as I could. "I know we don't know each other very well. But we are cousins. I'd like to know you better. And I really *would* like you to come tomorrow night."

Anne looked at me for a second. Then she said. "I couldn't. My mother wouldn't like it."

"Your mother wouldn't even have to know. She's been told to stay in bed for the next few days."

Just for a second, I thought I saw something wavering at the back of Anne's eyes. She has very pretty eyes, the colour of pale cornflowers, if only they didn't always look so dull and lifeless.

But then she shook her head again, the discontented look closing down over her features once more. "No.

I'm sure a closed carriage ride in the night air would be very bad for me. And besides, the Herrons don't know what sort of food I need. I mustn't eat anything rich or with too many spices or too much salt. It doesn't agree with me."

I gave up. "All right," I said. "But if you change your mind, let me know."

I had started to turn to go, but then my eye caught on the now closed window and I had a flash of how Anne had looked when I came into the room: teetering on the ledge, hands thrown out like the figurehead of a ship— or like someone about to throw themselves forward into space.

"Anne," I said. And for the first time I thought perhaps I should have left this to Elizabeth—or at least asked her to come with me—because she surely would know how to speak with Anne better than I. "You would not . . . you will not really try to . . . " I stopped, unsure of how to go on.

Anne turned and followed my gaze to the window. And then a thin, bitter little smile pulled at the corners of her mouth. "Don't worry Georgiana," she said without expression. "I haven't the courage for that, either."

Friday 6 May 1814

It's very late—or rather, very early. I have just heard the grandfather clock downstairs strike one in the morning. But I cannot sleep. Again.

We all went to the Herron's dinner party. Well, all of us except my Aunt de Bourgh and my cousin Anne. I kept hoping she might change her mind, but the hour kept getting later and later and still she stayed locked in her room. And finally just as we were gathering in the hall to depart, Dawson came with a message from Anne saying that she felt unwell and was going to take supper on a tray in her room.

I do wish I could have helped her more. But I could hardly stomp into her room, wrestle her into a gown and then drag her bodily into our waiting carriage.

So we set off: all the men of the party on horseback, just as I said, and Elizabeth, Caroline, and I in the carriage. Elizabeth had been looking a little pale again that morning, and when I offered her cold ham at breakfast she said, "Ugh, no—I mean, no thank you, Georgiana." But she looked much recovered tonight.

She was wearing a claret-coloured silk gown with lace at the neck and hem and the parure of pearls and rubies my brother gave her for a wedding present: bracelet, necklace, and a pearl and ruby studded comb in her hair.

Caroline looked very handsome, too, in a deep orange russet-coloured gown, with gold tassels at the sleeves and waist and a spray of feathers died to match in her hair. And I wore white: ivory-coloured silk with white flowers in my hair.

The Herrons are an older couple: one of those couples who have aged together until they look almost like twins: both rounded and with rosy faces and heads of curling grey hair. Though of course Mr. Herron was wearing black silk breeches and tailcoat and Mrs. Herron a green watered silk gown that made her look a little like a cabbage. But I should not say that—it sounds unkind, and I like her very much, I truly do.

The Herrons have three daughters and one son, all grown up and married now, and with families of their own. But Mrs. Herron always says she likes to be around young people. Actually what she said to me, laughing, was, "I get enough of seeing grey hair just by looking in my own mirror. Give me some bright young faces, that's what I say!"

So they'd invited most of the younger set in the neighbourhood, some familiar to me, others only in this area on visits.

One of those I did not know was a M. Jacques de La Courcelle, a French aristocrat who escaped the Reign of Terror with his life—by fleeing to England in a fishing boat, so he told us. With the recent overthrow of the Emperor, he has at last been able to recoup some of the property he left behind. And now he is staying at the Inn in Lambton while he looks about for a suitable estate to purchase.

He looks to be about thirty-five years of age. And he is very handsome in a sleek, olive-skinned way, with curling dark hair tumbling over his brow and heavy-lidded dark eyes. He is also very continental in his manners. When I spoke to him, I asked him whether he did not wish to return to France, rather than purchasing an estate here. He made a low bow and kissed my hand and said, "Ah, *chère Mademoiselle* , why should I wish to return to the land of my birth when there are sights as lovely as you in the land that has been my refuge?"

Caroline seemed very taken with him. She quite abandoned Mr. Carter and spent nearly the whole evening with M. de La Courcelle at her side. Though maybe that is lucky for Mr. Carter, since these last few days he has done almost nothing but blush and stammer and look thoroughly uncomfortable every time Caroline speaks with him.

The Herrons also had their granddaughter staying with them—Miss Maria Herron, the daughter of their only son. She is pretty—really, very pretty. Plump and round-cheeked and with black hair all curled in ringlets around her face. Mrs. Herron clearly adores her—and pushed Maria and me together from the start of the evening because we are so close in age.

When we were first introduced, Maria clutched both my hands and flashed a smile and said, "Oh, I'm *so* glad to know you, Miss Darcy! Or may I call you Georgiana? *Please* say that I may. I've been longing for someone to talk to! You can tell me all about the gentlemen in the neighbourhood. I'm *determined* that I shall not go back to my parents without being engaged, at the *very* least."

Her long-lashed dark eyes roamed over the company. "But *please* tell me if any belong especially to you, because I never, *never* poach other girls' particular young men."

Written all down like this, its sounds as though I am being catty. But I do not mean it that way. Actually, I spent most of the night wishing that I could dislike Maria. But I can't. Underneath all the giggling and batting her eyelashes and italics, she is good hearted and very sweet. And she is very fond of her grandparents— just as fond of them as they are of her.

It's just that unlike Elizabeth, who never makes me feel stupid or dull, even though I am so much more quiet in company than she is, Maria makes me feel as though I could—and should—fade into the wallpaper.

After my mother died, there would be times when I could not say a word in company with anyone I did not know. Not would not—literally could not. My throat would close up and my tongue would seem to freeze to the roof of my mouth and I would feel as though I could not breathe just at the thought of trying to speak.

That has not happened to me in years. And I suppose it did not *exactly* happen tonight. It was more like being under some spell in a fairy tale—the more laughing and vivacious Maria Herron was, the more I could feel myself freezing up and wishing I could be anywhere—*anywhere*—but there, in the Herrons' drawing room.

Before we went in to dinner, Maria pulled me into a corner and asked me who the *very* handsome gentleman in uniform was, because she adored soldiers *excessively*.

Edward was wearing his dress uniform: red coat with bars of gold braid.

I told her his name, Colonel Edward Fitzwilliam, and Maria said, "And he's not married, is he? *Please* don't tell me he already has a wife."

I said, "No, but—" but before I could finish with, *he is engaged*, Maria was off, heading straight for Edward and begging her grandfather—who was speaking to Edward at the time—to introduce her.

And from then on, throughout the whole rest of the evening, she attached herself to Edward and chattered away to him nonstop. They were seated together at dinner, and I could hear her asking him all about how he had been wounded.

I am not sure whether Edward actually told her. I have never known him to answer questions of that kind except by laughing and changing the subject. But he must have told Maria something, because I could hear her gasping and giving little exclamations of horror and saying how very *very* brave he must have been.

I have not even heard the story. I suppose that is partly because I have managed to almost entirely avoid speaking with Edward since the day of his arrival.

Though for his part, he has made it quite easy for me to avoid him. I don't think he has said more than three words to me these last few days.

No, that's not quite true. He asked me the morning

after he arrived, "How is your ankle this morning?" I said, "Much better." And he said, "I'm glad to hear it."

Which makes . . . what? eleven words, all together.

After dinner, Mrs. Herron proposed dancing, and I offered to play. Because playing—even in front of so many people—was so much better than being forced to watch Edward and Miss Herron dance. Of course she had claimed him for the first reel. And then—for I could hear them speaking together, even though I was staring so hard at my own fingers on the keyboard my eyes ached—every time Edward said that perhaps he would sit the next dance out, she clung to his arm and said, "Oh, no, please, you *mustn't* sit down. Not yet. You are such an *excessively* good dancer, and this reel is my *favourite*."

Finally, though, Elizabeth came over to me, saying that I must take a turn at dancing, and offered to take my place at the pianoforte. She would not let me refuse.

So I danced twice with Mr. Folliet, who dances very well, and once with Sir John Huntington, who has very damp, clammy hands. And once with Mr. Carter, who stepped on my feet three times. Though he felt much worse about it than I did, and kept stammering apologies, no matter how many times I told him it did not matter in the least. And three others of the gentlemen there, though I was introduced to them so quickly that their names are all jumbled together in my head.

I've just re-read that last paragraph, and it sounds as though I did not enjoy myself. But I truly did. I even forgot about Edward and Miss Maria. Mr. Folliet and the other three *were* very good dancers, and even Mr. Carter is so truly good and good-tempered that I couldn't help but enjoy my dance with him. Besides, it is a relief in a way to meet someone even shyer than I am.

And I actually love dancing, if I can get over worrying over having to make conversation with my dance partner.

I overheard two of Mr. Herron's younger footmen speaking together when they brought in more wine for the supper table. They were standing off in a corner, speaking in undertones of the women in the room, and one of them said that, "That Miss Darcy has turned into a right beauty and no mistake." And no wonder all the men were wanting a turn to dance with her.

Which I'm sure my aunt—or Caroline Bingley, for that matter—would have taken for impertinence. But I thought it was very nice of him. He didn't know I had overheard, so it was not as though he hoped to gain anything from the compliment. And he *could* have said instead that no wonder all the gentlemen wanted to dance with me, when I had a fortune of thirty thousand pounds.

I was going to sit down after that. But then Edward—just when I really had managed to almost forget about him—was there beside me, taking my hand and saying, "Georgiana, you must give me a dance."

I started automatically to pull my hand away, but Edward smiled one-sidedly and kept hold of me and said, "Have a heart, Georgiana. Miss Maria has gone to fetch her grandmother's evening medicine, but she'll be back in a minute. And if I don't have another partner, she'll tell me that whatever piece Elizabeth plays is her favourite, as well."

I laughed despite myself. "She's really very nice."

"She is," Edward agreed. He wiped his brow with the back of his hand. "That's just the trouble. You can't tell a perfectly nice, pleasant girl that she's making you feel like a ball being chased after by a bouncing puppy."

He was only asking me to dance as an excuse to get away from Maria. Which meant that if I had one single solitary scrap of pride, I ought to have refused. But it was exactly as though I had a little voice, whispering in my ear. In another month, Edward would be gone, off to marry Miss Graves. I might never have another chance of dancing with him, ever again.

So I left my hand in his and let him lead me onto the dance floor.

If I'd thought about it, he had given me the perfect chance to ask him about Miss Graves. Well, if I am honest, I *did* think of it.

I don't think he has mentioned her or his engagement at all since he arrived. Though of course, he may have spoken of it to my brother or Elizabeth without my hearing about it. And I did—just for a moment—feel the words hovering on my lips: *What about your betrothed? Surely you could just mention her to Miss Maria if you're looking for an excuse to get away?*

But I could not make myself speak the words. The music was playing, and Edward and I were moving through the dance. Every time he took my hand, I could feel the warmth of his fingers spreading all through me, like sunlight on my skin. My pulse was jumping in my veins. And there was a strange ache pooling in my heart.

"What are you thinking of?" Edward asked.

I realised with a jolt that I hadn't been paying attention to a single word he said. If he had said anything. I could not even be sure of whether he had been speaking to me or no. I jerked my head back up to look at him.

"Nothing."

The corners of Edward's eyes crinkled in another

smile. "It must have been quite some *nothing*. You were scowling like someone who's just seen a toad come hopping out from between the sheets on her bed."

His hand was still touching mine, still sending flickers of warmth down my arm, despite the fact that we were both wearing gloves. But it was no use, the spell was broken. I couldn't keep pretending he wasn't engaged to another girl. Or that he was dancing with me for any other reason than to sidestep Miss Maria's single-minded pursuit.

I put my hand up to my forehead. "I think . . . I think maybe I'd prefer not to dance anymore. I'm"—I cast about for some valid excuse for stopping in the middle of a set—"I think I'm feeling a little faint."

The smile was replaced at once by a look of concern. "Why didn't you say something? I wouldn't have asked you to dance if I'd known. Here—" I tried to protest, but already he'd put an arm around me and was half leading, half carrying me from the dance floor. "We should get you outside, out of all this heat and noise."

The room *was* hot. The evenings have turned warm, lately, and the heat and smoke of the candles made the air seem hazy and thick. Edward steered me out through the double French doors and into the garden outside. There was a stone bench near some rose bushes, and Edward led me to it and sat down, his arm still around my shoulders.

"Are you all right? How do you feel now? Can I get you anything—some wine, maybe?"

That of course is the trouble with inventing illnesses—you wind up being believed. What I really wanted, more than anything, was for him to go away and stop being so nice and thoughtful and concerned. There was a full moon out, turning the branches and leaves of the garden plants to silver, and the air was full of the drugged sweet scent of the early roses all around us, just beginning to bloom.

The entire setting, in fact, could not have been more romantic if a novelist had created it specially as a backdrop for her marriage-proposal scene.

Except that Edward was about as likely to propose as the moon was likely to turn into a bird and fly away.

"I'm fine," I said truthfully. "Not dizzy at all."

The hard, solid warmth of his arm about me was stirring up the ache in my heart all over again. I started to pull away. And then I realised that there were fine tremors running through the muscles of his arm and shoulder. And that despite the cooler air, there was a glitter of perspiration on his face.

"Are *you* all right, though?" I asked. "Is your arm paining you?"

"What this?" He nodded down at his shoulder. "No, it's fine. Whatever old Broyles gave me seems to have worked. I walked into Lambton this morning to see him, and he said I could leave off the sling any time."

"That is good news," I said. "And there is"—I hesitated—"there is nothing else wrong?"

Edward stared out into the moon-silvered garden. I thought at first he was not going to answer, but then he let out a slow breath and said, without looking at me, "I told you before it was . . . strange . . . to be back here, after a twelvemonth at war. Evenings like this"— he gestured back towards the house—"make it seem stranger still, I suppose. I don't—I'm not sure I fit in with it all anymore. Dancing—playing cards. Making polite conversation. It's been so long that I've almost forgotten how it's done. And then—" he seemed to search for words. "And then there's the heat . . . and the noise. That's what you remember most about battle. The incredible noise of it all—the roar of the guns, the shouting, the horses' screams. It's so loud it feels like a physical force, hammering against every nerve in your body. Being inside there"—he nodded at the drawing room windows again—"with the music playing and the room crowded and everyone talking at once. Even though it's nothing like battle, really—this still brings it all back somehow."

I felt another tremor run through his arm, and his hand clenched on the bench. But then he shook his head and said, in a different, easier tone, "All right. I've bared my soul. Now it's your turn. Do you want to tell me why the toad-in-the-bed scowl?"

I smiled. "You and my brother actually did put toads into Aunt de Bourgh's bed, remember? It was the summer we all stayed at Rosings Park for the whole of August, when you were both fourteen."

Edward tipped back his head and laughed. Some of the tension about the set of his shoulders seemed to ebb away. "I'd forgotten about that. How can you possibly remember it yourself? You were only—what?"

"Four," I said. "And of course I remember! That was the summer Aunt de Bough made up her mind it was time I learned to sew—she'd been keeping me at her side, hemming handkerchiefs from morning to dinner time, every day. But after she found the toads, she was too busy with ordering an entirely new set of bed linens and sheets to be bothered with me. You and Fitzwilliam were my heroes!"

"And your father gave us the thrashing of both our lives for it. It's astonishing he ever left your guardianship between the pair of us in his will."

"I don't know. I caught him the morning afterwards

standing near the stables, laughing so hard he practically had tears in his eyes. And besides," I added more softly. "He loved you. You know he did."

"I know." Edward looked down at me, moonlight reflecting silver in his dark eyes. "I'm sorry. I shouldn't have spoken of it."

"It's all right. It's been nearly seven years since he passed away." But despite myself, I felt a lump come up in my throat and tears prickle at the backs of my eyes.

It *has* been seven years. But even still, remembering times like the one we'd been speaking of—times when I'd no idea how short my time with him and my mother both was going to be—had brought it all back, somehow.

I swallowed. "I don't know why I said that—*passed away*. I hate that expression. Like *nourish*. That's another word I can't stand the sound of."

I was babbling, of course, but anything was better than bursting into tears now, in front of Edward. He must have endured much worse than I could ever know or dream of on campaign. The papers said that four thousand, five hundred of the allied troops died at Toulouse alone—he must have known some of them.

And yet even so, if I did start crying like a child of six, I knew he would either be nicer still to me—in an affectionate, older-brother sort of way, of course—or he would feel sorry for me, which would be worse.

Edward looked at me for a half moment. But then he raised one eyebrow and said, "All right. Tell me. What's wrong with *nourish*?"

"It's so sinister sounding! It's supposed to be a nice, wholesome word. But it sounds menacing—if you don't know its true definition, I mean. I think it's the *shhh* sound at the end. Have you ever noticed that? Words that end in *sh* sound malevolent, somehow. As though they were suppressing some vile secret."

Edward's lips were twitching. Which was better than feeling sorry for me. "So—*lavish*?"

"Yes, you see! Definitely sinister-sounding."

Edward's mouth twitched again, and then he gave up the struggle and laughed. "I'll have to remember that. If there's ever another war, and I'm facing a line of enemy cavalry, I'll yell out that I'm going to *nourish* them if they don't throw down their weapons."

I laughed, too. And then all at once we both stopped, as our eyes caught and held. It was just like that moment when he'd lifted me down from his horse. I couldn't move. I couldn't breathe. I couldn't even *want* to move or breathe. My skin was tingling, and I could feel my heart racing, so loud I was sure he'd be able to hear.

"Georgiana, I—" Edward stopped, his eyes still on mine. He rubbed a hand across his face. "God, this is insane, I—"

A footstep behind us made him break off and turn to look. It was Elizabeth and my brother. They must have been walking together in the garden and happened on us.

"Why, Edward—and Georgiana!" Elizabeth said.

"Are you all right?" I asked her. Because she had been feeling ill earlier today. I thought she really *might* have got dizzy with the heat inside.

"Oh, yes," Elizabeth said. She was holding onto my brother's arm and tilted her head back to smile up at him. "It's just that even so liberal-minded a couple as the Herrons would be shocked if they saw a couple dancing a waltz. A husband and wife, no less, dancing with each other! So I dragged your brother out here to dance in the moonlight."

A year ago, I think my brother would truly sooner

have been dunked in Pemberley's lake than been seen dancing out of doors, even just by Edward and me. And a waltz, yet—it is danced occasionally at balls in London, but even there it is considered quite shocking to see couples in each others' arms on the dance floor.

But he only smiled down at Elizabeth before turning back to Edward and me. "What are you two doing out here?" He looked from one of us to the other. "Is something wrong?"

Edward stood up. Stood up and stepped away from the bench so quickly he rapped his shin against a stone statuary and said a word under his breath I'm sure he does not usually allow himself in the presence of ladies. "Nothing serious. Georgiana was feeling the heat in there a bit, so I brought her outside for some fresh air. All right now?" Edward turned back to me.

I nodded. I could not quite manage to make myself speak yet.

"Good. I'll leave you in your brother and sister-in-law's capable charge, then. Thank you for giving me an alibi back there, by the way. And let me know if I can ever return the favour with any of the swarms of eligible young men panting at your heels. Though you've got Darcy here to play the stern elder brother. He ought to be enough to scare even the hardiest of unwanted suitors away."

And then he was gone, threading his way through the plants and back into the house.

I suppose he could have clapped me on the shoulder and said, *Jolly good, Georgiana, thanks for being such a good chum.*

Or patted me on the head.

Or said, *You know, Georgiana, you're almost like a sister to me. A sister. Let me say that just once more, in case you did not quite hear me the first time. You are like a younger sister to me, and I feel about you exactly the way an elder brother might.*

That would have been worse.

But aside from that, he could not have made his feelings any more clear. He's fond of me; he was grateful to me for giving him an excuse to get away from Maria. And I had probably just embarrassed him horribly by letting him see—again!—that I am completely in love with him.

Saturday 7 May 1814

My brother and Edward have been shut up in my brother's study since morning. It is afternoon, now.

I think a message in the morning post must have been the cause, because Fitzwilliam was halfway through opening his letters when he stopped abruptly with one communication in his hand and simply sat, staring at the words on the page.

My brother's expression is never very easy to read; I could not tell whether it was bad news or only something that bored him. He folded the letter deliberately in half and then asked Edward to come with him, because there was something he needed to speak to him about in private. And I thought, as Fitzwilliam spoke, that there was a flash of anger in his eyes.

Though whether he was angry at Edward or only at whatever the letter said, I could not tell.

I can't think what the message can have been about. Something Edward has done? But what? I cannot imagine Edward acting dishonourably. And it is not as though my brother is Edward's father, to call him to account for his behaviour.

They are still together in my brother's study, though; I could hear their voices when I went by. They were talking too quietly for me to make out the words, but they both sounded angry.

But let me think what else I can write about.

I have at long last made some progress with Anne, I think.

This morning after breakfast, we were sitting in the morning room, all together. Anne, Elizabeth, and I.

Caroline must have been quite taken with M. de La Courcelle, because first thing this morning, she volunteered to go into Lambton to pick up Aunt de Bourgh's medicine from the apothecary's shop. Dawson was wondering how the medicine was to be fetched, and Caroline practically snatched the prescription out of Dawson's hand.

Which is out of character enough for her that it made me think she wanted the excuse to take a carriage into town. M. de La Courcelle is staying at the Inn in Lambton, so he told us last night.

And then, too, Caroline came downstairs in her prettiest day dress, a pale green embroidered muslin, with a white straw bonnet trimmed with little bunches of scarlet poppies and green ribbon. And wearing her gold and silver embroidered cashmere shawl, despite the sky being grey and heavy with the threat of rain.

I only hope M. de La Courcelle is an honourable man. Since he has only been staying in the area a short while, no one seems to know very much about him, save what he told us himself at the Herrons' party: he has recently come into an inheritance and is looking about to purchase his own estate.

At any rate, Caroline was gone to Lambton and my aunt was still in her room. Anne was sitting in her usual

spot by the fireplace, bundled up in all her shawls—
and looking particularly sulky and bored. Because as
much as Anne resents her mother's constant harping
on her health, I suppose it is attention, of a kind. And
now Aunt de Bourgh has suddenly taken the place of
resident invalid, which leaves Anne without anyone to
fuss over her.

I sat down next to Anne, thinking maybe I could
draw her out. But after half a dozen attempts at starting
a conversation—and getting completely monosyllabic
replies: three *no*es, two *yes*es, and one muttered noise
of something in between—I was ready to grab Anne by
the shoulders and shake her.

Elizabeth was biting her lips with trying not to smile.
Not that she's not sorry for Anne, as well, because I
know she is. It's just she's so good at seeing the humor-
ous side of things.

I suppose it did look funny. Anne was sitting in a
high-backed settle and she wouldn't even turn to look
at me—so from the back it looked like I was trying to
hold a conversation with an unsociable armchair.

At any rate, just exchanging a look with Elizabeth
made me feel better. And on impulse, I picked up my
drawing things—pencils and crayons and paper—from
the table. I moved almost in front of Anne, or as close
to in front of her as the hearth would allow, and started
sketching her.

"What are you—" Anne started to say.

But I interrupted her. "Do not move—not even a
little bit! Just stay like that, exactly as you are."

One thing about living with my aunt, it has accustomed Anne to taking orders. She still looked sulky, but
she didn't argue. And she did settle back in the chair
and sat without moving while I drew.

After a while, she even stopped looking quite so discontented and started to look almost interested. She said—actually taking care not to move—"Will you let me see, when it's done?"

"Of course," I said. "You can see it now." I handed the drawing pad over to her. "It's only a rough sketch. I'll go back and fill in more details later—but I don't need you in front of me for that."

For a moment I wondered whether I'd made a mistake, because Anne just sat, quite still, looking for a moment at the drawing in her hand. Then she looked up. "This is me? I really look like this?"

"Of course it's you."

It was not a lie. Not really, because I had not altered her features at all, just smoothed out the bad-tempered lines around her forehead and mouth and made her look thoughtful instead of sulky and cross. The result was pretty—really very pretty, if I do say so myself. And she *could* look that way if she tried.

Anne sat there, looking from me to the picture and then back again. And then a small smile started to play about her mouth.

"Stay there! Just like that," I said. Because, smiling, Anne really did look as pretty as my drawing. Prettier, even. And then I had another flash of an idea. "Or no—wait, better yet, come out into the garden! The light is better out there, and you can pose for me on one of the benches."

I could see Anne wavering, undecided. "I might take a chill."

"No you won't. It's a beautiful day, all warm and sunny, you'll see. And we'll keep you well wrapped up in shawls. You won't be the slightest bit cold."

"Well—" Anne was looking up at the window.

"Come along. You can borrow my Spencer jacket, too."

I took Anne's hand and pulled her to her feet before she could protest any more.

I got her to wear one of my bonnets with a blue satin lining as well as the blue velvet Spencer, and the difference in her appearance was amazing.

Aunt de Bourgh sees that Anne is always dressed very well and very expensively, of course. But she always chooses the exact colours and patterns least flattering to Anne's colouring. Dull purple satins and heavy greens, and lots of busy patterns and gold braid. The dress Anne was wearing today was stripes of mustard yellow and burgundy that made my eyes hurt just to look at it.

The blue brought out the colour in her eyes and made her hair look like fine spun gold and her skin lily-pale instead of sallow. Before she could object, I dragged her out into the garden and sat her on a bench in front of some lilac bushes.

I was so absorbed in sketching that I did not hear Mr. Carter come up behind me until he cleared his throat.

"Oh, Mr. Carter." I turned around and smiled at him. "I've just been drawing my cousin Anne. What do you think?"

I held out the sketch pad, but Mr. Carter scarcely glanced at it. His eyes were fixed on Anne. "V-v-very nice," he said. Then he blushed to the roots of his tousled fair hair.

And then I had a *really* inspired idea. "What a lucky thing you happened to come by, Mr. Carter. I have just been wishing for a gentleman to pose with my cousin."

Mr. Carter hesitated. Anne was sitting close enough to hear us both, and I saw a frown start to wrinkle her brows. So I seized Mr. Carter's arm.

I did not know whether he was only shy, or whether a clergyman might think it improper to pose with a young, unmarried lady. He did join in the dancing last night, which would seem to show he is not overly strict in his views—but I wasn't going to take chances. Not with Anne about to fall into a fit of the sulks because she thought Mr. Carter did not *want* to pose with her.

"I wanted to draw . . . ah, . . . Joseph and Maria."

Mr. Carter looked at me blankly—as well he might, since I'd seized on the first two names that entered my head—and I hurried on, "They're characters from an opera. By, um, Mr. Henry Purcell. Joseph is Maria's brother, and in the scene I wanted to draw, he is comforting her on . . . on the loss of their beloved father."

Mr. Carter looked from me to Anne. "You w-w-wish me to pose as Miss Darcy—Maria's—brother?"

"Yes, exactly!" I was still holding his arm, and led him forward to Anne's bench. "Just sit right here beside her. Yes, that's right. Now, if you could just take her hand?"

At that precise moment, I looked up and saw that Mr. Folliet was standing behind the lilac bushes at Anne's back. Neither Anne nor Mr. Carter had seen him. And Mr. Folliet was looking as though he were going to burst into laughter at any moment. I made a face at him, willing him to be quiet, and turned back to Mr. Carter.

"Now , pretend that your father has died in . . . in the plague, and you're consoling your sister despite your own grief and your fear of the future. Yes, perfect!"

Mr. Carter actually looked far more nervous than grief-stricken—or comforting, for that matter. But he took one of Anne's hands in both of his, just as I had asked. And Anne actually smiled at him.

I stepped back and started to draw. Then—after waiting what seemed the bare minimum of time to make the claim believable, I stopped with an exclamation of dismay. "Oh, no! I've broken the tip on my pencil. And I've come out without my sharpening knife. Let me just run into the house to fetch it. You two stay right here, I won't be a moment."

I'm not entirely sure that Anne and Mr. Carter heard a word of what I said. But they did stay there, sitting together on the bench as I hurried away back towards the house in search of my mythical sharpening knife. Well, mythical in the sense that I had my *real* sharpening knife right there in my drawing box.

Mr. Folliet fell into step beside me before I had gone more than a hundred feet. He had moved away from the lilac bushes when I had made faces at him, but apparently he had not gone very far. His mouth was still turning up at the corners.

"Joseph and Maria?" he said. "Strangely enough, I've never heard of that opera."

"Really?" I said innocently. "Well, I suppose it *is* one of Mr. Purcell's lesser-known compositions."

"Is it indeed?"

Mr. Folliet flashed a smile, and I could not help but smile, as well. "Yes, a youthful effort, I understand," I said. "Not one of his best works."

We were both laughing by that time. Mr. Folliet offered me his arm, and I took it as we walked together towards the house.

Sunday 8 May 1814

Edward is gone.

He did not even say good-bye to me; I only learned of his departure this evening, when he did not come in to dinner. Elizabeth asked where he was, and my brother said, dividing his answer between Elizabeth and the rest of the dinner table, "I'm afraid I had some disquieting news. The youngest son of one of my tenants, old Mr. Merryweather down at Riggs Farm has decamped from his army regiment. Young John is a sergeant with the 11th Light Dragoons—it's a great grief to his father to see him abandon his duties. Edward has gone to see whether he can find the young man and talk sense into him before he gets himself into more serious trouble."

That *could* be true.

That could have been the nature of the letter that angered my brother yesterday morning—a communication from old Mr. Merryweather about his errant son.

And it would explain the conversation I overheard between my brother and Edward this morning. I was just finishing dressing, and they were walking past my door.

My brother said, "You'll take care of it?" He still sounded angry. "You'll have to find him first."

And Edward said, his voice harder than ever I'd heard from him before, "I'll find him. You may depend on it."

At the dinner table, Fitzwilliam did not hesitate, did not stammer or flush or even pause in giving his answer about where Edward had gone and why.

So why do I have the strongest feeling now that my brother was telling a deliberate untruth?

Monday 9 May 1814

My aunt got up from her bed for the first time today. And I should be glad that she is no longer ill. I *am* thankful that her illness was not more serious than a passing chill. But now that she is up and about once more, she is more determined than ever to see me safely engaged to one of her candidates.

Today she ordered us all to go out for a walk. A *very* long walk, she said, fixing me with an imperious eye.

Though Anne, of course, was not allowed to come and had to stay sitting in the morning room by her mother's side.

That is the other effect of my aunt's recovery—now that Aunt de Bourgh is no longer ill, Anne is firmly under her thumb once more.

Elizabeth begged off going on the walk, too, saying that she had a headache. I am beginning to be a little worried about her, she's had headaches or been otherwise indisposed so often of late. Though when I asked her whether she was truly ill, she laughed and said, wiggling her eyebrows, "You can't pretend with me, Georgiana. You're hoping I'll succumb to a wasting illness so that you can inherit . . . well, actually I can't think what I own that you might want to inherit. But I'm sure there's *something*."

As long as Elizabeth can tease and joke, there cannot be anything seriously—

I'm stalling. Writing on and on about my aunt and Anne and Elizabeth so that I will not have to write about what happened on the walk. Which is stupid. It's all over and done with. And yet somehow it has left a nasty feeling clinging to me like sticky cobwebs all over my skin.

With Anne ordered to stay home and Elizabeth's headache, it was just myself, Caroline, Mr. Carter, Mr. Folliet, and Sir John who went on the walk.

We started out on the path round the lake, all together at first. But then the path grew narrower. I can't even tell quite how it happened, but somehow when we had all shifted around, Caroline was walking in between Mr. Folliet and Mr. Carter, and Sir John and I were together, walking behind them.

At least I was not required to think up topics for conversation, because Sir John was perfectly content to do all the talking. He seemed intent on telling me about every single animal or bird he had ever shot in woods just like ours. *There was that rabbit two years ago—fattest fellow you ever saw. Got him with my second size double-barrel.*

And all he really wanted was for me to say, "Really?" or "How extraordinary!" every time he paused for effect.

He walked excruciatingly slowly, though—so slowly that almost before I knew it, Caroline and the other two men had drawn so far ahead of us that I could not see them any more around the twists and turns of the path. There was nothing I could do, though—I could hardly cut Sir John off in mid word and go sprinting off after them.

Well, actually, now that it is over, I wish I *had* done exactly that. But at the time I was just thinking darkly that I would not be surprised to see snails passing us on either side when I realised Sir John had paused again in whatever he had been saying.

"Really?" I said. "How perfectly extraordinary!"

Sir John gave me an odd look, and it was only then that I belatedly realised what it was he had said. I had been half listening without really realising it, and my mind had only just now registered the words: *You know, Miss Georgiana, I admire you immensely.*

My stomach lurched and my heart tried to drop into my boot soles. But before I could move or even think what to say, Sir John had taken hold of my hand. His prominent eyes were staring earnestly into mine.

"You'd make me very happy if you'd consent to be my wife."

I ought to have expected it, of course. I could imagine my aunt pulling him aside before we left and practically ordering him to propose. But it caught me off guard enough that I could not manage to frame a polite refusal, but just stood there, staring at him.

Sir John took my silence for hesitation. "I know we don't know one another very well. But all that's for after the wedding, eh?" He gave me a broad wink, then spread his arms. "Still, if there's anything you'd like to ask me before accepting, go right ahead. I'm a baronet—but you knew that already. Got an estate in Yorkshire. Once we're married, you'll be Lady Georgiana Huntington all right. And I've got a cracking fine stable, too, if you're keen on riding at all. In fact, I've got a nice little filly I picked up at auction last year that might just suit you, if you—"

Good heavens, I thought. Next he'll start talking about the guns in his collection.

He did not, as a matter of fact—he kept on with describing his estate in Yorkshire. But I could not stop expecting him to, and the thought of Sir John earnestly itemising his various fowling pieces as part of his marriage proposal made a bubble of hysterical laughter rise in my chest.

"And I'm a great huntsman, too. All in the name, eh?

*Hunt*ington. You'd never want for fresh game for the dinner table with me—"

It was too much. I must not have absorbed Edward's lessons from a year ago, because I found I still hated having to say no, even to Sir John Huntington. I was actually cold with nerves, trying to think of how I was going to break into all this flood of information and politely refuse him. And that, coupled with Sir John's assurance about fresh game made the laugh I had been trying to hold in come out in a very unladylike snort of mirth.

"Are you—are you laughing?" Sir John reared back, affronted, his brows instantly drawing together in a scowl.

I was. And what was worse, I could not stop myself. It was not even so very funny, it was more just nervousness and the sheer awkwardness of the whole situation that made it impossible to stop laughing once I had begun.

"Now see here." Sir John was still scowling. "Your aunt as good as told me that you'd undoubtedly accept my proposal if I were to make it today. Trying to make a fool of me, are you? See if you can string me along into proposing another two or three times before you finally deign to accept me?"

I stopped laughing. It was not funny at *all* any more. Sir John's grip on my hand had tightened painfully and his cheeks were darkening with anger.

"No, no," I stammered. "That's not it at all. I'm sorry, but I—"

"You teasing, spirited girls just need to be mastered, that's what it is." Sir John pulled me closer to him, slipping one of his arms around my waist.

I tried to pull away, but his hold on me was like iron. I was not *really* frightened. Reason told me—or should have—that he wouldn't actually assault me on the grounds of my own brother's estate. At worst, he'd manage to kiss me, after which I'd slap his face for him.

But his mouth was now inches from mine, and I realised from the reek of brandy on his breath that he must have been bolstering his courage before coming out on the walk. And the more I tried to wrench myself free, the more he only sneered and held me tighter still.

"Sir John." I did my best to sound commanding. "Let go of me at once!"

Sir John shook his head like a bull driving off an irritating fly and pulled me closer. I turned my head, at least, so that the kiss he'd meant to land on my mouth slid off my cheek, but I still felt his breath, moist and hot in my ear. "I'll show you a real man—"

And then all at once he was flying backwards through the air, landing spread-eagled on the mossy, leaf-strewn ground.

"I believe the lady asked you to release her," Mr. Folliet said.

Sir John's mouth was opening and closing like a fish gasping for air, but it was several seconds before any sound emerged. Then his face darkened again.

"So. Folliet here got in before me. I see how it is. You're already engaged to him, but the two of you cooked up this little stunt to make a fool out of me. Well, I'll show you." He looked from one of us to the other, his lips drawn back. "I'll show you who's a fool."

"Good. Why don't you do that," Mr. Folliet said pleasantly. He offered Sir John a hand, but Sir John scrambled up from the ground on his own. He threw one last, angry glance at us over his shoulder and then started off back towards the house, walking very fast and smacking viciously at the underbrush with his walking stick.

I drew in a shaky breath and straightened my bonnet, which Sir John's embraces had knocked askew. "Thank you," I said.

Mr. Folliet nodded. "Not at all."

My heart was still beating rapidly against my ribs. I drew another breath. "Not that I'm complaining, mind you, but how did you come to be here just now?"

Mr. Folliet shrugged. "I overheard your aunt speaking to Huntington before we all left and thought you might need a bit of rescuing at some point in the walk."

So it hadn't been just imagination—Aunt de Bourgh really had taken Sir John aside and ordered him to propose.

"Unless you really were just toying with Sir John and are of a mind to accept his proposal after all? In which case, I've not only robbed you of Sir John's company, but I'm afraid I've also just ruined your chances of becoming Lady Huntington for good."

He spoke lightly, still smiling, which helped combat the lingering unpleasantness of the scene with Sir John. I felt as though I could still smell Sir John's hot, brandy-reeking breath on my clothes.

"No, I promise you, I've no aspirations to being Lady Huntington," I said. "And I much prefer your company to Sir John's."

Mr. Folliet raised an eyebrow. "A dubious compliment, perhaps, to be preferred over an amorous drunken lout—but I will choose to be flattered, nonetheless. Will you walk on with me—or would you rather return to the house?"

I could feel my pulse gradually slowing. "No, I will come on with you. I would only have to face my aunt—or worse yet, Sir John himself—if I went back to the house now."

Mr. Folliet clapped a theatrical hand to his heart. "And I thought it was the irresistible appeal of my company you wanted. Crushed again. Still, I will not be disheartened—you have at least agreed to walk with me."

I laughed. "I will. Unless you decide to tell me that you are madly in love with me, too. In that case, I won't be responsible for my actions."

The moment the words left my mouth, I realised it wasn't the most tactful thing I could have said. "I'm sorry," I said quickly. "I'm just—"

Not that I imagine Mr. Folliet really is madly in love with me. A handsome, charming son of a very wealthy landowner in Kent—he must have girls everywhere setting their caps for him.

And as it happened, he waved my apology away with an easy smile. "No declarations of undying passion." He pretended to make a note in an imaginary book. "Right. Got it. You're safe now." He smiled again and offered me his arm, and we walked on. Over and past the bridge where I'd fallen the day Edward arrived.

Mr. Folliet looked more handsome than ever in a green riding jacket, buckskin breeches and gleaming black Hessian boots, with the spring sunshine bringing out russet tints in his dark hair. And when we reached the house, he even walked with me all the way up to the upstairs hallway, nearly to the door of my room, so that there was no chance of my meeting Sir John again alone.

It was very kind of him.

Tuesday 10 May 1814

Sir John Huntington departed the house this morning. I am so relieved.

I suppose I should not have felt so awkward about the prospect of being under the same roof with him—but I did, and I am so glad that I need not set eyes on him again. He did not even bother to invent some excuse for leaving, just told Fitzwilliam and Elizabeth that he wouldn't stay another night where he was no longer wanted, demanded his horses and curricle from the stables, and rode off.

Elizabeth was teasing me about it tonight after supper. My brother was sitting up late over some letter writing, and so Elizabeth came into my room, wrapped in her rose silk dressing gown, and perched on the edge of my bed while I brushed and braided my hair.

"That's two suitors you've successfully driven off," she said, laughing. "If you keep on this way, the house party will dwindle down to just ourselves before the next week is out. And then who will you dance with at the ball next week? Don't blame me if your aunt takes to advertising in the papers. *Wanted: any unmarried, eligible young men of good name and fortune. Must be willing to endure personal interrogation by none other than Lady Catherine de Bourgh.*"

She was very indignant, though, when I told her everything that had happened with Sir John.

"You should tell Darcy!" she said. "Or I will. The presumption Sir John had! Not to mention the abominable manners!"

"Tell my brother? Oh, no, please don't," I begged her. "He'd only be angry."

"He would probably ride after Sir John and take a

horsewhip to him," Elizabeth agreed. "And richly Sir John would deserve it, too."

"But I don't want him to!" I was getting alarmed, because Elizabeth's dark eyes were still fairly sparking with ire. "Please, don't tell him. I don't want any more unpleasantness. And anyway, Sir John is gone, and I'm sure he won't be back."

Elizabeth shook her head. "You are far too sweet-tempered and generous, Georgiana." Then, slowly her mouth started to curve upwards. "He really listed the horses in his stables and his skill as a huntsman as an inducement to accept him?" She was laughing by that time. "I thought I'd heard the height of absurd marriage proposals from Mr. Collins. But Sir John may have just established a standard of the ridiculous at which all other men may shoot in vain."

I started to laugh, as well. Now that it was all over, it was far easier to see the funny side of it again. Finally, Elizabeth shook her head and said, "All right. I will not tell Darcy about Sir John's behaviour, if you're sure that's what you wish. Does anyone else know?"

"Only Mr. Folliet. He was the one who stepped in and rescued me from Sir John, as I told you."

"Mr Folliet, yes," Elizabeth said. She adjusted the belt on her dressing gown and then said, carefully not looking at me, "He's very handsome, isn't he?"

I picked up one of the small pillows on the bed and threw it at her. "Stop! You're beginning to sound exactly like my aunt."

Elizabeth caught the pillow, laughing. "Heaven forbid! And all I said"—she widened her eyes in exaggerated innocence—"was that Mr. Folliet is very handsome."

"He is," I agreed. "Handsome and charming and

good-humoured. And kind, as well. And—"

I stopped. Mr. Folliet is, in fact, exactly the sort of man I *should* be able to fall in love with. Perfect in every single particular as far as I can tell.

And I look at him, and my heart does absolutely nothing at all.

It does not seem fair.

Wednesday 11 May 1814

I am afraid that Caroline really *is* smitten with M. de La Courcelle.

Why do I say 'afraid?' I am not even sure myself. We may not know much of him, but everything we do know is perfectly respectable. I will set what happened today down and try to decide whether I really do have cause for concern, or am only being fanciful.

Caroline begged me this morning to come into Lambton with her, because she had broken the lace on her boot and wanted to buy a new one. She may have broken a lace, but I do not believe that buying a new one can really have been the sole reason for her trip into town. It sounds uncharitable, but I do know Caroline. And being Caroline, she would far more likely have sent her lady's maid to buy the lace if she had not wanted to go into Lambton herself.

Once we were in the milliner's shop, she flitted from one item to another, picking up a pair of gloves, fingering a bolt of muslin, examining some dyed blue feathers, talking quickly and nervously all the while. *Thisisquiteprettydon'tyouthinkGeorgiana—Ohlookatthisitmightjustdoformygreenbonnet.*

And she kept stealing glances out the shop window as though she were hoping—or expecting—to see someone in the street outside.

She kept pressing me to try on bonnets and gloves and hold up bolts of fabric in front of the milliner's glass, as well. I did not want anything—after my aunt had her say about my wardrobe for this season, I have more clothes than three of me could wear—but eventually I gave way just to placate her.

I was trying on a straw bonnet with a ruched satin brim that Caroline had thrust into my hands and insisted would exactly suit me. And then when I turned around to tell Caroline that it was very pretty but I did not think I would buy it, she was gone. The shop was entirely empty, save for the milliner and myself.

I ran to the door—I am lucky that Mr. Jones, the shop owner has known me all my life, otherwise he might have thought I was trying to steal something—and looked out into the street, but Caroline was nowhere to be seen.

"If you are looking for your friend, Miss Darcy," Mr. Jones said, "she went out while you were tryin' that there bonnet on. She was looking out the window and must have seen an acquaintance of hers, because she bolted out of the shop like someone'd lit a fire under her and latched onto a gentleman out there in the street. I saw them go off together—that way." He gestured up the road.

I asked what the gentleman had looked like, and Mr. Jones frowned and polished his spectacles on the front of his smock. Mr. Jones is an old man—sixty, maybe—with white hair that grows in tufts over his ears, a bit like an owl. And he is very kind. I can remember him giving me sweets when I was small.

"Well, now. I don't see as well as I used to—eyes not being as young as they were. But he were tall. And he had dark hair. I did see that much."

That more or less settled the matter. It must have been M. de La Courcelle with whom Caroline went off.

She had gone without paying for her boot laces, too. So I paid Mr. Jones for them myself and waited while he wrapped them up into a parcel for me.

"Can't hardly believe you're a grown up young lady, now, Miss Darcy," Mr. Jones said as he folded the edges on the brown paper and cut a length of string. "Seems like only yesterday your good lady mother was bringing you in here." His eyes had gone distant behind the lenses of his spectacles. "Ah, she were a rare fine lady, were Lady Anne Darcy. There's many a woman of her rank as wouldn't be seen buying from a simple country shopkeeper like me. But she always said my muslins were as good as any she could get in London and better, as often as not."

That was true. My mother always bought from the merchants in Lambton and Kympton; she said she would far rather pay her money to those who lived about us and whose faces and families she knew than some rich London tradesman she knew not at all.

"And the poor of the parish loved her, too—and with good cause, for Lady Anne did a fair bit of good amongst them," Mr. Jones went on. "Many's the time I've seen her going to visit a poor family with the wife a widow or the husband sick in bed."

That was true, too, and it pricked my conscience, because there are several poor families my mother helped and took an interest in, and I have not visited them as much as I ought of late, what with spending so much of this past year in London and only coming down to Pemberley a few weeks ago for my aunt's visit.

"Ah, she's missed, is Lady Anne Darcy, she's missed

around these parts still." Mr. Jones tied off the string with a neat knot and handed me over the parcel. "Still, the new Mrs. Darcy, your brother's wife, looks to be another such as Lady Anne was. A very nice young lady, we all think her. If it's not an impertinence to say so."

"I'm sure Elizabeth will be very glad to hear it," I told Mr. Jones. "And I'm sure she'll be in to your shop herself before too long."

Before we parted, Mr. Jones gave me a handful of peppermint candies. "Because I remember how partial to them you always were when you were small."

I actually detest peppermints—if I ate them before, it was only because I was too shy to refuse. But I would never hurt Mr. Jones's feelings, so I put one in my mouth and thanked him and said my good-byes.

And then I went out into the street to look for Caroline.

There was no sign of her. I walked all up and down Lambton's market street and looked into every single shop, from the confectioners to the tiny lending library on the corner. I even looked into the butchers shop, where Caroline could have had no earthly reason to go unless she discovered a sudden urgent need for a rack of mutton or lamb.

But Caroline was nowhere to be seen, and neither was M. de La Courcelle. I had asked Jem, our coachman, to meet me at the Rose and Crown Inn. And it was there—after what must have been more than an hour of searching—that I finally found Caroline. She was coming out of the stable yard, where the inn keeps its carriages and horses for hire.

Caroline's cheeks were flushed and her eyes were bright and she gasped when she saw me—then tried to pretend she had been searching for me all along. "Oh,

there you are Georgiana! What on earth's kept you?
You've been such ages."

"*I've* been such ages? You ran out of Mr. Jones's shop
without even paying!"

At least Caroline had the grace to blush at that; the
flush on her cheeks deepened. "Oh, well, I—thought
I saw an acquaintance in the street. But I was . . . mistaken. Then by the time I'd got back to the milliner's
shop, you'd gone. So I came on here to wait for you."

I was tempted to say that anyone who can not tell
lies better than that should give up trying. But Caroline
looked really happy, which is more than I've seen her
look in months, and I hated to be the one to try to
dampen her spirits.

So instead I only said, "This acquaintance wouldn't
happen to have been M. de La Courcelle, would it?"

Caroline tossed her head. "It might be—or it might
not." Then she lowered her voice and took me by the
arm, pulling me towards the coach that Jem had by that
time brought round to the front of the inn. "Can you
keep a secret, Georgiana? If I tell you something, will
you swear not to tell a single soul?"

"Well—" but it didn't really matter what I said. She
was too bursting with the news to keep it to herself,
though she waited until we were safely inside the carriage and rolling and jouncing back over the roads towards Pemberley.

"M. de La Courcelle took me to see the estate that
he is thinking of buying! He said he wanted a woman's
opinion on it before settling the matter and asked me
to come and look at it. He hired a horse and carriage
for the ride from the Rose and Crown—that was when I
met you outside the stable yard, we'd just got back."

"A house?" I was so surprised I scarcely knew how

to reply. "And M. de La Courcelle took you to see it this morning?"

Caroline nodded. "Yes, it's a big old stone-built place to the north of here, just past the village of Kympton. Do you know it?"

I nodded slowly. "I think so. It must be Kennelwood Hall, I think, it's the only property of that size and description near Kympton."

"Kennelwood. Yes, I believe that was what Jacques— M. de La Courcelle—called it. It's a beautiful old place." Caroline was still speaking so quickly that the words fairly tumbled out. "Old fashioned, of course, but as I told M. de La Courcelle, you could soon put that to rights. Dig up the garden—maybe put in a lake. And maybe build a conservatory onto the house—there's plenty of room for one, if you were to cut down some trees."

I was frowning. "But Kennelwood Hall belongs to the Duke of Claridge," I said. "He's hardly ever in these parts, for he spends most of the year on his estates in Hampshire. But even so, I hadn't heard that he intended to sell Kennelwood. And," I added, "why should it be a secret that M. de La Courcelle wants to buy it? He could just as easily have called at Pemberley and arranged a proper outing if he was so anxious for you to see it."

Caroline sniffed. "Honestly, Georgiana, you've no sense of adventure! M. de La Courcelle only learned today that the property was for sale, and he couldn't wait—he wanted to see it at once! And as for secrets, it appears there's another buyer interested in the property. Jacques—M. de La Courcelle—doesn't want this other buyer to hear of his own interest, for fear the other buyer will get a bid in ahead of him." She sighed. "It's so cruelly unfair! M. de La Courcelle has only been able to recoup a bare tenth of all his family once owned. They were once one of the most wealthy families in all France. Now all the rest of his family are dead, fallen to the guillotine. And Jacques is reduced to surviving on only a fraction of the riches he was born to."

I managed not to point out that a man contemplating buying Kennelwood Hall is hardly to be pitied for his poverty.

"Are you—" I hesitated. I *did* hate to be a damper on Caroline's good spirits. But I said, "Are you sure it's . . . wise, to go about alone with M. de La Courcelle, when we've only just made his acquaintance? And unchaperoned?"

Caroline tossed her head again. "We were not unchaperoned. M. de La Courcelle's manservant was with us, to see to the horses. There was nothing improper. Well—" She smiled a small, secret little smile, colour coming into her cheeks again. "Not much improper, at any rate."

Caroline certainly knows her own mind. And then, too, she is hardly likely to accept advice from me or anyone else. Still, I couldn't stop myself from saying, "You will take care, won't you Caroline? Don't do anything reckless or hasty?"

"Why not?" A line of temper appeared between Caroline's brows. "I think I would rather like to be reckless and daring for a change. Besides, it's all very well for you to talk, Georgiana. *You're* monopolising the only handsome man staying at Pemberley."

"Mr. Folliet?" Despite myself, I could feel my cheeks colouring. "He's very agreeable. But I don't mean to . . . to monopolise him, I promise you. And besides, there's Mr. Carter—"

I'd hoped he and Anne might really strike up a better

acquaintance, but now that my Aunt de Bourgh is up and about again, Anne seems to have lapsed into all her old ways. She's scarcely spoken a word to anyone this last day or so.

"Mr. Carter!" Caroline sniffed. "As if I'd want a stammering parson for a suitor!" I started to protest that Mr. Carter was very nice, and intelligent, as well, but the lines of temper on Caroline's face only deepened. "Oh, do leave me alone, Georgiana!" she said crossly. "And stop lecturing me. Do you not think I deserve to be happy?"

Thursday 12 May 1814

I spoke to Elizabeth about Caroline last night. Elizabeth said she will speak to my brother Fitzwilliam about writing to Charles—that is, Charles Bingley, Caroline's brother. He and Fitzwilliam between them will make enquiries about M. de La Courcelle.

I suppose Caroline will be very angry with me when she finds out. But I feel much easier knowing that someone besides me is aware of her association with M. de La Courcelle. And sooner or later Elizabeth and my brother would have learned of it in any case, because this morning Caroline slipped out of the house very early, before anyone else but the servants was awake.

She told Mrs. Reynolds, our housekeeper, that she was only going out into the garden to cut some flowers for the breakfast table. But that cannot have been true, because breakfast time came and went and there were no flowers—nor any sign of Caroline, either. She did not come back until well past one o'clock in the afternoon.

Her dress was all stained with grass and dirt—she was wearing a white muslin with a blue sash, and every mark showed plain. But she only said that she had gone for a walk and had lost her footing and fallen. Luckily for her one of the cottagers on the estate took her in and let her rest awhile and gave her a drink of water from their well.

She had one ankle all wrapped up in rags, just as mine was last week. The cottager had done it for her, she said.

But she has not been limping at all. Or rather, she limps only when anyone asks her how her ankle is. And when I asked her for the family name of the cottager who had helped her—so that we could offer him and his family some suitable thanks—Caroline only looked blank and said she had not asked him for his name.

No other news. And no word of Edward, wherever it is he has gone.

Friday 13 May 1814

A (small) miracle has occurred: I actually managed to drag my cousin Anne out of the house again today. I *was* pleased, because it seemed as though even the small amount of progress I had made with her while my aunt was ill was doomed to go to waste. But until today, I could not think of a way of prying her away from Aunt de Bourgh again—unless it was by slipping a dose of sleeping medicine or syrup of ipecac into my aunt's morning tea. Which might have been effective, but too unkind a trick to play, even on Aunt de Bourgh.

It was Caroline who finally put the idea into my head with her talk of the cottager yesterday. I mightn't believe that she encountered any such person on her walk—unless M. de La Courcelle has decided against Kennelwood Hall and bought a cottage on my brother's estate instead.

But there *are* in fact several families that I have been meaning to visit, as Mr. Jones reminded me in Lambton the other day. And this morning looked to be perfect weather for it; when I got out of bed, the morning sky outside my window was clear blue, streaked with the gold of the sunrise.

My Aunt de Bourgh often stays abed late in the morning, on account of her sleeping so poorly at night. Often she does not come down to breakfast at all, but only takes tea and a tray of dry toast in her room.

So first thing, as soon as I was dressed, I went along to my cousin Anne's room. She was dressed, as well, in a morning dress of twilled olive green silk, the hem double-flounced and the sleeves ruched and the whole dripping with so many yards of lace that Anne's slight frame was almost entirely lost to sight.

Her lady's maid—a young, scared-looking girl named Janet—was just brushing Anne's hair, and Anne was saying fretfully that Janet must take care to be more gentle, else she would give Anne a headache.

After I had told Anne good morning, I said, without any preamble, "I'm going to ask Mrs. Reynolds to make up a hamper of jellies and jars of broth so that I can take them round to the poor families in the parish. Will you come with me?"

"Go out? And among the *poor*?" Anne looked at me as though I had just asked her whether she wouldn't like to strip down to her shift and go for a roll in the home farm pig pen. "I mean, I couldn't possibly."

"Which part couldn't you possibly do?" I asked her. "Go out of the house? Or give food to those who haven't enough to eat?"

"Both . . . either. I mean, I'm sorry for them, of

course." Anne sounded sulky. "But my mother always pays tithes to our parish church at home, you know, and—"

"There you are, then," I interrupted her. "I'm sure your mother would approve of your extending the reach of her charitable work by visiting the poor here."

Anne's eyes darted back and forth as though she were looking for some means of escape. "I . . . I think I might be going to have a headache," she muttered.

"Oh, for heaven's sakes, Anne," I said, exasperated. "Is that honestly how you want to spend your day today? Sitting in your room here alone and trying to decide whether you're going to have a headache or not?"

Without even entirely meaning to, I looked at the bedroom window, the same window I'd found Anne kneeling in front of, all those days ago.

Anne followed my gaze—and whether it was the reminder of that day or just sheer boredom I don't know, but she hesitated another moment then said, still sounding sulky, "All right, I'll come. But it will be your fault if I take a chill."

I asked Jem to bring the horses and carriage around to the front of the house again, because some of the families I wanted to visit live too far even for me to walk, much less Anne. And we had the food hamper Mrs. Reynolds had prepared to carry, besides.

Despite the sunshine, Anne insisted on wearing her warmest pelisse, a hideous garment made of mustard yellow velvet and lined with dark sable fur. She had a matching sable muff, as well, to tuck her hands inside. But she did get into the carriage with me without any argument—and she didn't even complain that Jem had brought out the barouche instead of the closed carriage— and left the top on the barouche down, besides, so that we rode in the open air.

It is only in fiction, I think, that the poor are more honest or noble than the richer classes, or that their cottages are quaint and picturesque. They are not at all.

But I do like all the families we visited. Even the two Miss Abdy's, who are a pair of unmarried, elderly sisters and the most prying, avid gossips in the village. Before I had left the small, rented lodgings they share over the butchers' shop, I'd heard all about which boys had pilfered chickens from which hen yards and which husbands were spending all their week's wages on drink at the Rose and Crown and knocking their wives down when they came home.

Anne wouldn't come in with me to any of the cottages, but waited in the carriage while I paid my calls and left jars of calf's-foot jelly and jars of beef broth everywhere we stopped. Finally we came to the last name on my list, old Mrs. Tate, who lives in a tiny, down-at-heels cottage on the outskirts of Lambton. She used to make a little money selling herbs and simples to the villagers for cures. Though the rheumatism in her hands and legs has made it harder and harder for her to dig in the garden.

And she has grown a bit forgetful, besides, so that her cures tend to be more hazardous than helpful to take. I know Mr. Broom, the village apothecary has had to be summoned to quite a number of her customers who have felt the full effects of one of her tonics.

Mrs. Tate was outside when we drove up, and she hobbled over to the side of the barouche to greet us. She is a tiny figure, much bent and wizened, with a leathery, wrinkled face and an almost toothless mouth. She was wearing a brown skirt and bodice so ancient as to be almost worn through in places, and a blue kerchief on her head, with a few wisps of snowy white hair straying out from under the kerchief's edges. Her eyes, though, have somehow stayed almost young-looking. They are dark dark brown, bright and keen and very shrewd.

"And when are we going to hear the bells rung for your wedding, Miss Georgiana?" she asked me after we'd exchanged all our greetings. "Pretty girl like you must have the men round her like flies on the jam pot. Though mind"—she winked at me—"doesn't do to give any man what he wants too easily, like. Start as you mean to go on, I say, and unless you mean to let your husband have his way all the years you're married, don't say 'yes' when he asks, 'will you?' right away." She nodded her head. "I had three husbands, you know. And every one of 'em would come to heel when I called, right enough. Though"—she winked again—"of course there do be ways of keeping a man in line once you've wedded him that I shouldn't speak of to a pair of unmarried misses like you. Wonderful what just the threat of separate beds will do to a man."

I nearly choked trying to swallow a startled gasp of laughter, and beside me I heard Anne gasp outright. Mrs. Tate smiled broadly—and toothlessly—at both of us. And when I had my voice back, I asked her how she was faring these days.

Mrs. Tate bobbed her head and lifted a gnarled, age-spotted hand. "Ah, well, can't complain, can't complain. Still alive, and with a roof over my head and two sticks to make a fire on cold nights, and that's a sight better than some in this world. And I've got my garden." She nodded behind her at the tiny plot of turned earth set against the cottage's northern wall. "Seems like a body can't help but be happy if she's got good, rich soil to root around in and make things grow from." And then she peered from me to Anne. "And who's this, then, Miss Georgiana? Friend of yours?"

"My cousin, Anne de Bourgh," I told her. I had assumed Anne would die of horror if I tried to introduce someone of Mrs. Tate's lowly rank to her. But as it happened, Anne utterly shocked me by making Mrs. Tate a little half-bow, half-nod of her head and saying, "How do you do."

Mrs. Tate looked her up and down. "Well, now, you are a little thing, aren't you? And kind of peaky-looking." She peered into Anne's face. "In a little un, I'd say the mother ought to eat a mouse every morning for a month. But someone your age . . . I'll tell you what." Mrs. Tate bobbed her head decisively again. "You come back here in a week's time, and I'll have a tonic made up for you of hawthorn berries. That'll soon put some colour in your cheeks."

Anne actually said, "Thank you," and Mrs. Tate smiled again, clearly pleased. "You come along, too, Miss Georgiana," she said to me. "And I'll show the both of you a love charm for catching the man of your choosing. You just bake a little cake or something sweet—with your own hands, mind—and spit in the batter while you're stirring it up, and say the words I'll tell you. And just like that"—she snapped two fingers together—"the man you give it to will be yours for life."

Anne was very quiet as we drove back towards Pemberley, and I looked at her a little anxiously. She *had* taken more fresh air and sun today than she likely has in this last month put together.

"Are you feeling all right, Anne?" I asked her. "You haven't got a headache, have you?"

"Just don't try to tell my mother that she ought to eat mice for breakfast," Anne said.

I looked at her, astonished. Because in all the years I have known Anne, I have never known her to make a joke. I was not even certain she was making one now.

Anne was smiling, though—so she had indeed meant to be funny. Then she said, "Will you let me come back here again with you?"

"To Mrs. Tate's?" I asked. I was surprised. "Why? For the hawthorn berry tonic?"

"Actually it was the trick of spitting into a cake-batter love charm that I wanted to learn," Anne said, with a perfectly straight face.

And then we both started to laugh. When Anne had finally stopped, she wiped her eyes with the edge of her fur muff and said, a little hesitantly, "No, really, Georgiana, I would like to come out with you again. To all of the families you saw. May I, the next time you go to visit them?"

So actually I suppose that makes two miracles that occurred today.

Saturday 14 May 1814

The Herrons and Miss Maria came to a dinner party here tonight; the reciprocal visit in thanks for their hospitality last week. M. de La Courcelle was invited, too.

Elizabeth came to my room while I was dressing to tell me that M. de La Courcelle would be present. She looked even lovelier than usual in a new gown, a peach silk with an overdress of ivory net, trimmed all round the hem with deep pink satin rosebuds.

When she told me about M. de La Courcelle, I asked her whether she was certain that was wise. Elizabeth frowned, unusually serious. "Your brother wants the chance to speak with him and know him better," she said. "Darcy is an excellent judge of character"—she smiled fleetingly—"his tendency towards hasty first impressions aside." Then she sobered. "No one here has any authority over Caroline," she said. "We can write to her brother, but their parents are dead, and she's a grown woman. We can't forbid her to see M. de La Courcelle. And she can leave Pemberley at any time if she doesn't like it here. Much better to give her legitimate chances for seeing M. de La Courcelle. Flouting convention is all very well, but she may do herself serious harm if she keeps slipping off to see him in secret."

Elizabeth is right, of course. And as it happened, M. de La Courcelle and Caroline were together for very little of the evening.

With Edward gone, Maria was forced to devote her attentions to Mr. Folliet and M. de La Courcelle equally, chattering to them, asking them to dance with her in turns.

That sounds spiteful now that I have written it down—though it did not in my head. Words are strange that way, aren't they? Your own thoughts can sound unfamiliar and strange when they are out there, spoken in the world, as though they have taken on a life of their own.

But I do like Maria Herron, actually. There was real friendliness and warmth in her greeting to me—and she'd brought both Elizabeth and me little gifts, as well, of needle cases she had sewn herself. I told her I would make a drawing of her in return, and she seemed truly thrilled.

M. de La Courcelle, when he was not with Maria, was making himself agreeable to the rest of the party. He *is* very charming, I suppose. I had offered to play the pianoforte so that the others might dance, and M. de

La Courcelle came over to me and bowed over my hand, clicking his heels together smartly. "But why should a young lady so charming as yourself be consigned to spend the evening here, slaving at the keyboard to entertain us all? Surely your sister-in-law so *agréable* would favour us with her playing so that you may dance instead of work."

I had a French governess when I was small—and of course, we were taught French at school. So I smiled and said, in his own tongue, "Le travail éloigne de nous trois grands maux: l'ennui, le vice et le besoin." Meaning, of course, *Work delivers us from three great evils: boredom, vice and want.*

M. de La Courcelle looked at me blankly for a moment. Then he said, "Ah, but alas, *chère Mademoiselle* , I have sworn never again to speak the language of the land that has betrayed me and broken my heart." He clapped a hand to his breast. "From now on, I speak the good King's English alone. The English of my adopted home. Though I assure you"—he took my hand again—"if anything could rekindle my love for my mother tongue, it would be to hear it on the lips of you, Mademoiselle Darcy."

I was tempted to ask him for more details about the Revolution, out of a sort of morbid curiosity to see whether he could turn talk of the guillotines, too, into extravagant compliments. But I only smiled and nodded, and he left me with another low bow.

I suppose a French aristocrat might not be expected to appreciate quotations about the value of work.

After that, M. de La Courcelle devoted himself to my Aunt de Bourgh. He seemed to be laying himself out to be especially charming to her. So charming, indeed, that I wondered for a moment whether he had made a mistake in the relationships and thought that Caroline was my aunt's niece or daughter. Or whether he had decided to abandon Caroline entirely and make a play for Anne.

Caroline has a fortune of her own, but it is nothing to the inheritance Anne will have. And if what Caroline told me about M. de La Courcelle's reduced fortunes is true, I cannot imagine he would not prefer to have Anne's.

Which also sounds spiteful. I suppose I should not be biased against him. For all I know, M. de La Courcelle may be sincerely attached to Caroline.

But he *did* devote himself very attentively to my Aunt de Bourgh. He sat beside her throughout the latter half of the dancing, and must have spent a quarter of an hour at least adjusting the fire screen to her liking. Though the days have been warm, the nights are chilly, still, and my aunt has insisted on fires in the grate every night since she recovered from her cold.

I should have thought she would have small patience with M. de La Courcelle's heel clicking and hand kissing, but she actually seemed to enjoy his company. They spoke together for quite some little time, and twice at least I saw Aunt de Bourgh smile at something M. de La Courcelle had said. Which is doubly surprising, because—as I suppose I might have expected—my aunt has not been in the best of tempers since Sir John Huntington's departure.

I have not told Aunt de Bourgh that I outright refused Sir John. I'm despising myself for cowardice even writing this. But she was furious enough about his departure already without my telling her the whole tale. She has of course realised that a match between us is not likely, though, and has told me several times in freezing tones that it must surely be my fault.

And then I compounded the sin by taking Anne out with me yesterday.

Aunt de Bourgh read me a little lecture on the subject yesterday evening, of which the words *feckless, hoydenish behaviour* were the mildest terms she used to describe what I had done.

Since she usually lectures me for being too shy, I could have pointed out that I can't be a wallflower and a hoyden, both. But I doubt it would have served any purpose except to make her angrier still.

And as much as I may indeed despise myself for cowardice, my hands felt clammy at the thought of prolonging the scene with her.

At least M. de La Courcelle's attentions to Aunt de Bourgh tonight left Anne free for much of the evening. Aunt de Bourgh didn't even order Anne to bed when the clock chimed nine.

I saw Mr. Carter go over to Anne and ask her if she would care to dance. Anne hesitated, then darted a quick glance at her mother's back—Aunt de Bourgh was facing away from the dance floor—and regretfully shook her head. Mr. Carter sat down beside her, though, and stayed there talking with her all the rest of the night.

They were sitting near the pianoforte, so that I was nearer to them than anyone else in the room, and I overheard Mr. Carter say, when I was taking out some new music to play, "I'm m-m-much obliged to you, Miss de Bourgh, and so are all the partners whose feet I would have stepped on if I'd joined in the dance." And then he coloured. "I'm afraid that came out wrong. I didn't mean to imply that I was merely looking for an excuse not to dance. I . . . I enjoyed talking to you very much,

Miss de Bourgh."

And then I realised that I was nearly falling off the pianoforte bench trying to overhear Anne's reply. I could not catch all the words, but I think it was something like, "Thank you, Mr. Carter. I've enjoyed your company, as well."

Monday 16 May 1814

There was a letter this morning for my brother from Edward; I saw it lying beside Fitzwilliam's plate on the breakfast table when I came down. But I have scarcely had time to think of it or even wonder about what he said.

I am sure Aunt de Bourgh would hardly be pleased at my regarding what has happened in terms of my own inconvenience. Though—something else I would not have expected—I really am very sorry for her.

I would be even more sorry for her if she had not upset the servants so much. Joan, one of the chamber maids, just came into my room to draw the curtains and rake out the fire in the grate, and she was still sniffling and red-eyed. Though at least the house is quiet, now that the physician has been and given Aunt de Bourgh something to make her sleep. I would not have believed it possible in a place as spacious as Pemberley, but all the morning, the entire place seemed to echo with my aunt's screams.

But I've just re-read what I've written so far, and I seem to be making no sense at all. I suppose the morning's events have left everyone off balance.

I had just come down to breakfast—and recognised Edward's hand on the topmost letter in my brother's pile of morning messages—when a high, keening scream sounded from one of the bedrooms upstairs.

I was sure someone must have been hurt, though I could not tell who. I couldn't recognise the voice, and even when I'd run upstairs and found that the screams were coming from my Aunt de Bourgh's room, I couldn't believe it was she who was making such an outcry, for I'd never heard my aunt sound like that before.

The door was half open, so I went inside, and found my brother and Elizabeth there before me, one on either side of Aunt de Bourgh. She was still screaming. Though now that I was inside the room, I could make out a few words. "Theft! Robbery! My pearls!"

Elizabeth put an arm around her. For all Aunt de Bourgh has always been so horrible to her, Elizabeth was as kind as could be. She asked me to run down and fetch a glass of brandy, and once I had brought it back, she put it to my aunt's lips and coaxed her to drink.

"That's right," Elizabeth murmured, when Aunt de Bourgh had taken a few swallows from the glass and her ragged breathing had slowed. "Now, please try to tell us what's the matter."

My aunt had recovered herself at least a little by that time, for she shrugged off Elizabeth's touch and spoke to my brother.

"You must search the servants' quarters at once!" Her voice was quivering, though with anger, not tears. "I demand it. And see that they are questioned, too. I have never liked the look of that chamber maid—the girl who comes in the mornings to start the fire. She has a sly, insolent look in her eyes."

That is poor Joan, who is a truly sweet, good-hearted girl, but born a little simple in her wits, so that she is more like a child of five than a woman of twenty or twenty-one. Her worst enemy—though I cannot imagine her even having one—would not call her sly.

My brother raised his eyebrows, but said, very patiently, "If you could just tell us what all this is about, Aunt?"

Aunt de Bourgh drew in a long breath and took another swallow of the brandy and then did finally consent to explain.

It seems that when they spoke last night, M. de La Courcelle admired a pearl and garnet ring that my aunt was wearing. He's something of an expert on antique jewellery, or so Aunt de Bourgh said. Before the revolution, he was making a study of the many historic jewels that had been passed down in his family. Though now that the collection has been almost entirely lost, he makes a hobby of studying and sketching any jewels of particular history or interest he comes across.

Since he had admired the ring so much, Aunt de Bourgh thought to show him the pearl necklace that is part of the same matched set, one that has been in her family since it was made for a distant ancestress during the reign of Charles I. But when my aunt opened her jewellery box this morning to take out the pearl necklace, she found it gone.

"Some good-for-nothing, dishonest wretch has clearly stolen it," she finished, holding out the empty velvet pouch where the pearls were kept. "So I demand you organise a search of the house. The necklace must still be here—there has not been time for the culprit to have made an escape."

I had been standing by the door, and I am not sure my aunt even realised fully that I was in the room. But I said, "You think the necklace was taken by one of the servants, Aunt?"

Aunt de Bourgh sniffed and drew her brows together.

"Of course. One can never entirely trust members of that class. The chamber maid—"

I can probably count on the fingers of one hand the number of times I have spoken out of turn in my aunt's presence, still less ventured to interrupt her. She has a way of fixing you with a look that seems to stab clear through to the bone, and always makes me feel as though the words were rocks lodged in my throat.

At least it's not only me. I remember her lawyer, Mr. Evens, visiting her once when I was at Rosings Park. He is a silver-haired gentleman, very stately and dignified, and Aunt de Bourgh reduced him almost to tears.

Still, I broke in to say, "Have you searched the room? Surely it's possible you may only have misplaced the necklace?"

Aunt de Bourgh gave me a withering look and sniffed again. "*You* may search the room if you wish, Georgiana. *I* am going to demand of your brother that he interrogate his servants and search their quarters. I want no door or drawer left unopened until my pearls are found!"

Elizabeth and I hunted about the bedroom together while my brother continued to speak with my aunt and rang the bell to summon Mrs. Reynolds. Elizabeth was still very calm and collected as we looked behind the big clothes press and opened drawers and even looked under the bed. But she looked worried, all the same, with an anxious furrow between her brows.

"What are we going to do if the necklace really has been stolen, Georgiana?" she asked me. "It will be horrible enough if it really was one of the servants. But even worse if the necklace can't be found and they all of them have to go about with the suspicion of the crime attached to them."

I had not any answer to that—I have not still. And all our searching of my aunt's bedroom turned up only dust and an old, chipped button that must have broken off someone's dress and rolled under the bed.

By the time we were finished, Mrs. Reynolds had answered my brother's summons. She was splendid. She faced Aunt de Bourgh without flinching and said that there wasn't a single servant on staff here at Pemberley whose character she wouldn't vouch for. My brother said the same, but said that since he wasn't going to have any doubts cast on his servants' honesty, he would see that the search my aunt demanded was made, if only to prove her wrong.

Which I suppose it did. Prove her wrong, I mean, for the servant's wing has been searched, and all the other rooms of the house besides, and there's still no sign of my aunt's pearls.

I think my aunt would have liked to go on raging at the servants herself, but my brother stopped her and told her she was only upsetting herself and should retire to her room while he summoned the physician.

And that was when I did start to feel sorry—truly sorry—for Aunt de Bourgh. Those pearls have been in her family for generations, and she was very proud of them. And maybe their being stolen isn't much of a tragedy in the larger scheme of things, but it is a tragedy to her. And one that Aunt de Bourgh has been ill-prepared to meet, since she is so accustomed to always being able to order the world to her own specifications.

I remember Edward once vowing—and I do not even think he was teasing me—that he once heard Aunt de Bourgh say in the summertime that she was most displeased by the lack of rain and would have to speak to someone about it. And Edward laughed and said that he assumed by 'someone' she meant God, and that he could just see Aunt de Bourgh including a stern lecture on the summer weather in her evening prayers.

I'm not sure I am explaining myself very well. It's just that it seems to me that what is a terrible hardship to one person may seem trivially small to another, but that does not necessarily make the hardship any the less hard to bear for the one who suffers it.

Elizabeth and I both went with Aunt de Bourgh to her room and helped her to unlace her stays and lie down while we waited for the physician to arrive. And she really had exhausted herself with anger, because she scarcely protested at all. Her face was all grey-tinged and her mouth drooped, and she looked ten years older than she had at dinner last night.

After Mr. Roberts, the physician, had come and given my aunt a dose of laudanum, I offered to sit with her until she fell asleep. But Elizabeth shook her head.

"You had better see if you can go and soothe down the servants, Georgiana" she said. "They've all known you for far longer than they have me. And we don't want them all giving notice and leaving because of this upset."

Aunt de Bourgh was almost asleep, her eyes half-closed, but she still murmured fretfully and turned her head against the pillow. Elizabeth put a hand on my aunt's forehead and spoke softly and soothingly until she quieted.

My brother had come into the room to see how my aunt did, and he put an arm around Elizabeth, kissed her forehead, and said, "You're an angel. You know that?"

Elizabeth leaned against him, but then she smiled and said, "Oh, no. Impudent and headstrong as ever.

I'm just lulling you into a false sense of security, that's all."

I did speak to the servants and assured them that we didn't suspect any of them of wrongdoing. Except—my aunt's necklace *is* missing. And who did take it?

My brother questioned everyone in the house, and I asked a few questions of Mrs. Reynolds and the upstairs maids, too. But no one seems to have seen anything; no one observed an intruder creeping into my aunt's chambers or anything of that kind. My aunt could not remember definitely when she last saw the necklace. It was kept inside the velvet pouch, which was kept inside her jewellery box. And the velvet pouch was left behind, so that she may not have realised the pearls were gone for some days.

But she thinks that she last opened the pouch and saw the pearls sometime before—

Oh. Oh my.

I remember once I was standing in the morning room during an autumn storm. The force of the gale blew the garden door open when I was standing in front of it and hit me with an icy gust of rain.

The idea that's struck me as I sit here writing this now felt just the same.

I think I may know exactly who stole Aunt de Bourgh's pearls.

The only trouble is that now I am going to have to nerve myself to tell Aunt de Bourgh.

Tuesday 17 May 1814

I have done it.

I went to my aunt's room first thing this morning and told her my theory about who had stolen her pearls. I may be a coward about defying Aunt de Bourgh—but I could not let suspicion fall on an innocent person. And I must say, my aunt took the news far better than I had expected she might.

She was sitting up in bed when I entered, still in her nightdress and lace cap. Beneath the cap, her hair still hung down in its nighttime braids. Her eyes were still a little heavy, I suppose with the effects of the laudanum, and just for that moment, I could see a fleeting glimpse of how she must have looked when she was young. She must have been very handsome.

Then she straightened and rapped out a "Well, Georgiana?" and the impression shattered.

I drew in my breath and willed myself not to sound nervous while I told her the whole of the episode of Sir John's proposal. Every unpleasant detail; I forced myself to leave nothing out.

"He said, at the last, *I'll show you who's a fool*," I finished. "And I may of course be wrong. But I think Sir John was the one who stole your pearls, Aunt. You said yesterday that you'd last seen the pearls on the night before Sir John's departure from Pemberley. I think he must have slipped into your room sometime on the morning he left and taken your necklace as a means of revenge on both of us. Me for refusing him, and you for . . . " I stopped, trying to think of a way to put it that would not give offence. "For encouraging him to propose," I finally finished.

I had braced myself for anger, recriminations, even renewed screams—in short, for my aunt to hold me to blame for the loss of her pearls.

Instead she listened in silence, then when I had finished, she nodded her head decidedly. "You were quite right to refuse him, Georgiana," she said. "Such manners! Such low-breeding. I had expected better things from Old Sir John Huntington's son. However," she pushed back the coverlet and sat up straighter. "However, I shall write his mother a strongly-worded letter about her son's behaviour. You may fetch me my writing box, Georgiana. I will have the letter ready to mail by breakfast time, and one of your brother's menservants may take it into town to be mailed without delay." A small, grim smile touched the edges of her mouth, "Lady Arianna Huntington is an old acquaintance of mine. I make no doubt she will see to it that her son returns my pearls without delay. She will make his life unfit for living until he does."

Aunt de Bourgh's letter has now been written and safely posted. I've had the occasional small twinge of conscience for fear I am mistaken, and Sir John didn't take the pearls after all. But then, I suppose Sir John is more than capable of defending himself if he is innocent. And to be honest, if I am right and he is guilty, I am relieved to have the matter so easily resolved.

Without mentioning names—because of course we *do not* have definite proof of Sir John's guilt—my brother gave the servants to understand that they were not under suspicion. He asked them not to speak of the theft, but some of them must have, for M. de La Courcelle came to pay a call this afternoon. He had heard of the theft in town from the barman at the Rose and Crown and come at once to pay his condolences on my aunt's so-grievous loss, or so he said.

"Ah, *chère Madame* ," he said, bowing low over Aunt de Bourgh's hand. "What courage you have in the face of such a blow. Truly, you are an inspiration to any of us poor mortals who have suffered at the hands of Fate."

Elizabeth and I were sitting with my aunt in the drawing room during M. de La Courcelle's call, and I did not dare even glance in Elizabeth's direction for fear she would make me start to laugh. Aunt de Bourgh inclined her head and thanked M. de La Courcelle very graciously, though.

I wonder why he really came to call.

Though maybe I am being unfair again. Maybe M. de La Courcelle is simply one of those unfortunate people who sound like frauds even when they're being perfectly sincere.

He can't have come to see Caroline—or at least I don't think he can, since he did not seem disappointed in the slightest to hear she had gone out. Caroline had persuaded Mr. Carter and Mr. Folliet to walk into Lambton with her, I am sure in the hopes of seeing M. de La Courcelle. She, on the other hand, will be wild with disappointment when she learns that he actually came to Pemberley while she was gone.

Oh, and I very nearly forgot. I finally managed to speak to my brother and ask what news Edward had sent in his letter. But there was nothing, really, of note. Edward hasn't yet succeeded in finding Mr. Merryweather's son. But he hopes to have settled the matter in time to return for the ball at Pemberley in two weeks.

Wednesday 18 May 1814

Have I mentioned the intended ball yet? I suppose perhaps I have not. Without entirely meaning to, I have been avoiding even thinking about the subject, much less writing about it.

My aunt insists that my brother and Elizabeth give a ball here at Pemberley in my honour. I have never had a grand ball to mark my entrance into society, she says, though I was presented at Court last year.

Of course, my brother would have refused if I had asked him to. But it seemed too selfish and ungrateful to refuse when he was offering to host a ball just for my pleasure. I know he is not over-fond of such occasions, but for my sake he was perfectly willing to host one here at Pemberley. And then, too, I knew Elizabeth would love the idea of a ball here, because it gives her a chance to invite her parents and younger sisters to stay.

She misses Kitty and Mary a great deal now that she lives so far apart from them. And Kitty, of course, is already engaged to be married. But I know Elizabeth would like to give her sister Mary the chance of finding a match, as well.

And even her father, who is decidedly not over-fond of travelling, would be forced to make the journey to Pemberley for an occasion like a ball. I think Elizabeth misses her father most of all.

At any rate, I agreed to a ball being given here in two weeks. Though I confess I'm dreading it more than looking forward to the night.

I *do* love dancing. I even like going to balls. It's just the thought of one being given in my honour . . . of so many eyes being on me throughout the evening . . . of having to talk to so many people I don't know very well, and having the whole assembly of guests look on while I lead in the first dance that makes me feel ice-cold.

But none of this is actually the reason I set out to write about the ball today. It was because I found my cousin Anne crying this morning.

I had got up and gone downstairs earlier than usual so that I might spend an hour or two practising the pianoforte. But when I opened the door to the music room, I heard a rustle of fabric and a quick, unevenly drawn breath. My heart jumped, for I was remembering the loss of my aunt's pearls and thought that perhaps there had been an intruder, after all—and now the intruder had returned.

But then I saw my cousin Anne, curled up on a chair in a corner of the room with her eyes red and her face all splotchy and tear-stained.

"Why, Anne, whatever is the matter?" I asked her. "Are you ill?"

Anne shook her head and scrubbed furiously at her eyes. "No." Her voice was a ragged whisper. "No. I'm not ill. Just . . . just go away, Georgiana. I'm perfectly well."

Perhaps a month ago, I might have gone away as she asked. But not now. Instead I dragged the pianoforte bench over and sat down beside her. "You don't look perfectly well to me," I said. "Please, Anne. Won't you tell me what's wrong? Maybe there's something I can do to help."

Anne stiffened and for a moment I thought she was going to order me away again. But then her thin shoulders drooped and she brushed again at her cheeks. "Very well. I'll tell you." Her head lifted, and she blinked angrily at me, her eyes still swimming. "And then you can laugh at me for being so foolish. I want to dance at the ball."

I was startled. But Anne's voice had broken on a fresh burst of crying, so I put my hand on her arm. "I don't think that's foolish," I said. "But I don't understand. Why shouldn't you dance at the ball if you want to?"

Anne looked down at the floor again, and said, her voice so low and uneven I scarcely heard her. "I don't know how to dance."

"You don't—"

"No! I don't know how to dance. I never learned." A bitter note crept into Anne's tone. "My mother wouldn't hear of it—she said it would be too taxing for me and that I mustn't tire myself with trying."

"Let me teach you, then."

Anne's head lifted again and she looked at me in astonishment. "What?"

I had spoken on impulse, without stopping to think. And because the thought of Anne, twenty-eight years old and never summoning the will to insist on learning to dance had made my skin prickle with a sudden chill.

But it seemed more and more possible, even when I considered the idea. "Let me teach you," I said. "We've thirteen days until the ball is held. I'm sure I can teach you at least some of the more common figures in that time."

Anne was still blinking at me, and I could see the indecision wavering behind her reddened eyes. "Well," she said.

"Come." I stood up and held out my hand to her. "We've an hour before anyone is likely to come into this part of the house. I'll teach you the figures for a quadrille first. If you can master that, you can master them all."

To my surprise, Anne actually agreed—I had thought it would take far more persuading than that. But she stood up and followed my instructions as we went through the steps. *Coupe balote, glissade, pas de basque*, and all the rest.

We went through the quadrille three times, and Anne did very well—which also surprised me, though I tried not to let it show. She is actually very graceful when she isn't huddling up under rugs and shawls. And she did not even seem tired at the end, only a little out of breath and flushed.

"Meet me here again tomorrow morning at the same time," I told Anne when we parted, "and I'll teach you the steps to the cotillion."

And Anne agreed to that, as well.

Thursday 19 May 1814

Mr. Folliet has been enlisted into helping with Anne's dancing lessons. I realised yesterday afternoon that Anne would need to practice with music before she is truly ready to dance at a ball. And since I cannot partner her and play the pianoforte at the same time—and since I do not really know the men's part of the dances very well in any case—I spoke to Mr. Folliet last night after dinner.

My aunt had retired to her room to write letters, so she said. I think she intends on writing her lawyer, Sir John' Huntington's mother—and likely anyone else she can think of—every day until she secures the return of her pearls. And Caroline had gone to her room, as well. With a headache, so she said.

Elizabeth was playing and singing for us, and my brother had eyes only for her. Anne and Mr. Carter were speaking quietly together.

And I drew Mr. Folliet to the windows. "If I ask a favour of you," I began, "will you promise me not to speak of it to anyone else?" And then realising that sounded more than a little forward, I hurried on, "It's not a favour for myself—at least, not really. And it's nothing improper, I promise you."

One of Mr. Folliet's eyebrows rose, but he smiled a little and said, "I assure you, the possibility of any impropriety never even entered my mind. And how could I refuse a request as intriguing as this one?" He placed a hand over his heart and made me a little bow. "I promise you, tell me whatever it is you need, and my lips are sealed."

"Oh, thank you!" I let out a breath of relief. "That's why I asked you. I knew you could be depended on. It's my cousin Anne. She wishes to learn to dance."

Both Mr. Folliet's eyebrows went up this time. But he listened while I explained the whole to him. And when I had finished he assured me gravely that he would happily join Anne and me in the music room—risking Lady Catherine de Bourgh's displeasure and his toes being trodden on—so that my cousin might have the pleasure of dancing at the ball.

For all his good-natured teasing, Mr. Folliet did come to the music room this morning. Actually he was there even before Anne and myself, already waiting when we went down. Wearing his evening pumps instead of boots, which was very foresightful. And he was utterly kind and patient with Anne in leading her through the steps of both the cotillion and the quadrille, while I played the piano for them.

We practised for over an hour, and when we had finished, Mr. Folliet bowed and said to Anne, "You are a natural dancer, Miss de Bourgh. If you'll permit me to say so."

Anne's cheeks were already flushed with the exercise, but they went pinker still at the compliment. She stammered out a shy thanks, and then Mr. Folliet said, "There's a masquerade ball to be held at the Lambton assembly rooms in two days' time. What do you think of attending?" He looked from me to Anne. "Both of you. It would give Miss de Bourgh the chance of practising in company. And anonymously. More or less. All those in attendance will be masked."

Anne's jaw dropped open at the very thought of attending such a function. "I don't know . . . that is, I'm not sure . . . "

I had not really expected her to say yes; I was astonished that we had managed to draw her into dancing in the privacy of the music room.

Mr. Folliet only said, though, that we needn't decide

at once, and could make up our minds tomorrow.

I haven't done much sketching of late. But here are
Anne and Mr. Folliet, going through the steps of the
quadrille.

Friday 20 May 1814

If the writing of this entry looks like a drunken, ink-
covered spider has wandered over my pages, it's because
my hands haven't entirely stopped shaking yet.

George Wickham is here. Here at Pemberley, I mean.

A part of me had always been bracing myself for having to see him again sometime. Because after all, he is married to Elizabeth's sister.

But Elizabeth always said that she would never have Lydia or Wickham here at Pemberley. For one thing, she would not be answerable for what my brother might do if Wickham ever set foot on the grounds again. And for another, Elizabeth said she would be far too tempted to shake Lydia until her teeth rattled.

Wickham is here, now, though. And I do not think that anything could have prepared me for the shock of seeing him again.

Mr. Folliet, Anne, and I had just finished our morning's practice in the music room and were crossing the foyer to the breakfast room for the morning meal. I was happy, too, because Anne really *is* doing quite well with the dancing. She smiled and laughed and talked to Mr. Folliet as they danced today—and afterwards she said she was starving and wasn't it breakfast time yet? That is another change in her: the last day or two, I've noticed at table that she has actually eaten her meals instead of only picking listlessly at the food.

At any rate, just as we were passing my brother's study, the door opened and George Wickham stepped out.

I was so shocked I stopped dead and Anne bumped into me from behind. I could not move. I felt as though I had been forcibly detached from my body and was watching myself from a long way off as George said, with a faint echo of his old, charming smile, "Ah, Georgiana. How delightful to see you again."

He even tried to take my hand and kiss it, but I recovered myself in time to yank it back before he could raise it to his lips.

He has changed. Not 'so much that I wouldn't have recognised him,' as they always say in novels; nothing so dramatic as that. But he *has* changed very much. He was wearing his army uniform, red coat and tan breeches. But where he was once muscular and broad-shouldered, he's grown paunchy. His corn-coloured hair is now thinning on top, and his face has grown puffy, with lines of dissolution about his eyes and mouth.

I think he had been drinking, despite the early hour, for he reeled back shakily when I pulled my hand away and had to steady himself against the wall, shaking his head as though to clear it.

I think he might have said more, but my brother appeared in the doorway behind Wickham.

Fitzwilliam does not often lose his temper. All the time I was growing up, I do not think I ever heard him raise his voice; when he is very angry, he gets cold and quiet rather than loud.

He was *very* angry this morning. Not that it showed much, save in the tight line of his jaw. "We have an understanding," he said, very softly to Wickham. "Now get out of my house."

Wickham wobbled unsteadily around to face him. "You might have put that more amiably, Darcy, old friend. Yes, indeed you might. A man less generous-spirited than myself might be inclined to take offence at your tone. However"—he drew himself up with a little swagger and replaced his black officer's hat on his head—"however, to demonstrate the perfect amiability which I hope will mark all our future relations, I shall do as you ask. Georgiana,"—he made me a bow—"I hope to see you soon again."

Saturday 21 May 1814

If George Wickham's arrival is what the old gypsy woman meant all those nights ago by telling me an old love would return, I feel at the moment as though I could ride alone into their encampment and demand a refund of the coins I paid her. Or tell her that she is in need of spectacles for her second sight, or whatever it is she calls her powers.

I am a little surprised that my hands are not shaking again as I write this, for what happened today was worse than merely seeing George Wickham again. But my hands are quite steady, strangely enough.

It is seven o'clock in the evening, and I am dressed for the masquerade ball as a queen: a long red velvet cloak for a royal robe and a crown of primroses in my hair. The costume did not take long to put on, so I have a few minutes to sit down at my bedroom table and write this.

Today I woke early and went out alone into the garden before breakfast. It was a beautiful day, with the warmth almost of summer in the air, and I'd taken my sketching book outside to draw in the garden. I had barely begun to pencil in the outlines of my picture—I was going to draw the rose trellis, just breaking into a tumble of blooms—when a shadow fell across my page.

I was expecting Elizabeth—or maybe Mr. Folliet, since I had seen him come outside a little while before. But when I looked up, it was George Wickham I saw standing over me. I gasped and drew back instinctively, and an unpleasant smile tightened the edges of his mouth. "Ah, I see. Too proud to associate with me now, Georgiana?" he said. "I remember a time when you liked me well enough. That summer at Ramsgate? You weren't so high and mighty in your tastes, then. Now you've set your sights towards grander things, though, eh? The son of your father's steward isn't good enough for you?"

He had been drinking again. He was leaning over me, and I could smell the liquor on his breath. It was like a nightmare repetition of Sir John's proposal, almost. But worse—much worse—because as much changed as Wickham was, I could still feel myself slipping and sliding backwards in time as I looked at him. Not towards falling in love or infatuation with him, I don't mean that. But sliding back into being that girl I was three years ago, the one who had been so lacking in confidence, so much afraid of issuing a refusal, that she had been intimidated nearly into an elopement.

I stood up and said, as steadily as I could, "I assure you, Mr. Wickham, that your parentage never did concern me in the least. And if you were a son of the King himself, now, I would still not wish to have any further acquaintance with you. Please, leave me."

Wickham swayed unsteadily and then lurched forwards, towards me. I tried to step back, but he seized hold of my wrist, his eyes focusing blearily on my face.

It was then I realised he was even more intoxicated than I had thought. Far more so than Sir John had been. I had never been around real drunkenness before, and a prickle of cold fear started to spread outwards all through me. The rose garden is some little distance from the house, and I didn't see another soul anywhere close by; I was not even sure anyone would hear me if I screamed.

"A little bird told me you were likely to be soon engaged—and to an earl's nephew," Wickham went on.

He must have meant Mr. Folliet, of course. There are no other earls' nephews staying at Pemberley. But before I could deny it or ask where Wickham could have heard such a rumour, his grip tightened and his fingers dug into my arm. "But it's not going to happen. The old earl's not going to want his nephew marrying a baggage who was on the brink of marriage to me, a lowly steward's son." Wickham shook his head and then leaned forward confidingly. "Been having some money troubles, you see. Cards haven't been lucky for me of late—not lucky at all. And my lovely wife"—his mouth twisted on the word—"likes spending money, you know. That's when I hit on this scheme. Get your brother to pay me for my silence. I wrote him—but he didn't send the money as I asked. So I came on here to Pemberley. After all, I ought to be paid something. You owe me. You and your brother both." His lips were almost touching my ear. "Never breathed a word to anyone about our little love affair, Georgiana. Never a word that might sully your reputation."

I felt as though I had been kicked in the stomach. My whole body flashed cold, and I could not seem to draw in a full breath. And then a red-hot wave of anger seemed to spread all through me. I could almost feel it hissing through my veins. Because of course I realised now what that letter to my brother had really contained. And where Edward had actually gone.

Miraculously, though, I was not frightened any longer. I jerked my arm out of Wickham's grasp, then put both hands on his chest and shoved as hard as I could.

If he had not been so far gone in drunkenness, I would never have managed to make him fall. But as it was, he was so unsteady on his feet that my push sent him over backwards, sprawling and crashing down onto one of the rose bushes.

Wickham was roaring and swearing—I'm sure the thorns were scratching him very painfully indeed—and thrashing around, trying to get up. But I did not wait to see whether he would manage it, or even look back. I was already on my way up to the house and my brother's study.

Edward was there, too; he and Fitzwilliam were speaking together and they both started and looked round when I flung open the door. Edward was in dusty and sweat-stained riding gear. He must have been tracking George Wickham ever since he left, and only this morning traced Wickham back to Pemberley. But at that moment, I was too angry to feel surprise at his presence or even care that he had returned.

"Georgiana, what—" my brother began. He looked alarmed, but I would not let him finish.

"It was a lie," I said. "About old Mr. Merryweather's son. He never abandoned his regiment at all. George Wickham tried to blackmail you, and you sent Edward to deal with him. And you never told me!"

Fitzwilliam and Edward exchanged a look. Then my brother said, "I thought only to spare you the pain of—"

But I interrupted him again. "You should have told me! No matter how painful it might have been. I am not a child. And the matter concerns me—it is my reputation Wickham is threatening. And I had to hear it from him instead of from my own brother!"

Fitzwilliam's face darkened at that. "Wickham is here?" He sounded as close to losing his temper as I have ever heard him.

"Yes, in the garden, I—"

Edward was already gone, striding past me out the

study door. I'm sure on his way to the garden and Wickham. But he did not even glance at me as he passed. His shoulders were set and a muscle was jumping in the line of his jaw.

"Georgiana, please let me—" my brother began as the door closed behind Edward.

But all at once I didn't want to hear any more. Couldn't *bear* to hear any more, actually. I could feel a hot press of tears behind my eyes and a lump in my throat—and that would have been the final, impossible humiliation, if I had broken down then and there and sobbed like a child.

I turned and ran out of the study. Ran up the stairs and to my bedroom, shut and locked the door. I did think for a moment about throwing myself on the bed and indulging in a fit of tears. But it would have been just as childish to cry in private as in my brother's study.

So I made myself draw a long, slow breath, splashed water from the washbasin on my face, and then went to Anne's room and went in without bothering to knock.

Anne was lying on the chaise—her mother always insists on her lying down for a rest in the middle of the day—wearing a silk dressing gown and with a little satin pillow filled with lavender seeds resting over her eyes.

"We are going to the masquerade ball tonight," I said.

Anne started up. The lavender scented pillow slid to the floor with a soft thump. Anne blinked at me. "Georgiana, what in the world—"

If I had been in a better temper, I might have found the number of speakers I seemed to be interrupting in mid-sentence a little funny. As it was, I did not care about that, either.

"The masquerade ball," I said. "The one at the Lambton assembly rooms that Mr. Folliet spoke of. We are both going to attend."

Anne's hands went nervously to the neck of her dressing gown. "Georgiana, I couldn't possibly attend . . . I mean to say, a function of that kind . . . my mother would be so angry if I went—"

"Yes," I agreed. "I'm sure she will be very angry indeed if you attend. And if you don't attend, you can turn thirty years of age secure in the knowledge that you never once made your mother angry by following your own wishes or living your own life. But apart from that, I don't see what is to be gained by always doing exactly as she says."

Anne's mouth formed a perfect round O at my tone. But she didn't speak.

I do love my brother. He is all the close family I have, and everything that is kind and good in an elder brother. I do wish he had told me of Wickham's threats. Though now that I have had time to think, I cannot say that I entirely blame him for failing to do so—he is my guardian, as well as my brother. Charged by our father to see to my protection. I know he meant for the best, and to spare me pain.

It's not really him I was—am—so angry with, but rather myself. For so very nearly being swayed and intimidated into an elopement with Wickham. For not asking my brother for the truth in the first place when I suspected he was lying about where Edward had gone. For not standing up to my Aunt de Bourgh and being afraid of refusing Sir John Huntington and . . .

I suppose that that is really why I have been so determined to help my cousin Anne. Because, apart from the fact that her mother is Lady Catherine de Bourgh, she and I are in so many ways exactly the same.

"There are some old pantomime costumes and gowns of my mother's stored upstairs in the old nursery rooms," I told Anne before she could say any more. "We can surely find something in the way of masquerade attire for both of us."

I am not sure even now whether Anne truly wanted to find masquerade costumes, or whether she simply thought I had taken leave of my senses and ought to be humoured. But she did come upstairs with me. The nursery rooms have not been used since I was small, of course, and they have turned into an attic of sorts where all the old or broken or disused things are kept. Old-fashioned, heavily carved wardrobes and dressers. A broken spinning wheel. Hat boxes and an old wooden cradle that I remember using as a bed for my dolls.

Some of my old dolls were actually still sitting on the shelves, and the ball and Bilbo cups my mother and I used to play with.

And pushed up against one of the gable windows were a couple of trunks with pantomime costumes and old clothes. There was no dust—Mrs. Reynolds is far too thorough a housekeeper for that. And all the clothes were packed with cedar blocks to keep the moths away.

Anne and I set to looking through them all. And if Anne had come upstairs just to humour me, she soon began to enjoy herself. It's been years since we had any pantomimes or dressing up at Pemberley, so I had not seen the old things in ages. Papier-mâché masks, painted in silver and gold. Spanish lace shawls. A blue velvet doublet, the sleeves slashed with red satin. A black domino costume: hooded cape with an attached black mask.

It took some time for us to find something that would

fit Anne, she is so very thin and small. But finally in the bottom of one of the trunks, I came across an old-fashioned, long-waisted gown in buttercup yellow satin with inset panels of white satin trimmed with tiny pink flowers. I think it must have belonged to a very young girl, for it looked as though it would fit Anne exactly.

"Look, Anne!" I held the dress up for her to see. "It's perfect—it might have been made for you."

I could see Anne wavering again as she studied the dress. "What would I be meant to be?"

"You can be a shepherdess," I said. "We'll fix your hair in curls and find you a crook." I turned up the hem of the yellow gown. "There's enough fabric here in the facing to trim a bonnet—you can borrow one of mine, if you like. I've a white straw that would look well with this yellow. And you can wear this mask." I held up one of the eye masks, a white one with little spangles of gold set over the brows.

Anne hesitated. But her fingers were already moving almost of their own accord to stroke the full skirt of the gown. It *was* beautiful: the elbow-length sleeves trimmed with three flounces of lace and the neck and bodice ruffled with lace, besides.

"You could at least try it on," I told Anne. "Look, there's an old mirror over there in the corner. And you're still wearing your dressing gown. We can see how it looks on you right here."

I helped her into the gown, tying the laces, doing up the dozens of tiny hooks that attached the bodice to the skirt. Then I stepped back and drew in my breath. That sounds silly, but I really did, the change in Anne's appearance was so complete.

Anne looked at me nervously. "How do I look?" she asked.

"Come and see for yourself." I tugged her to the mirror.

Anne turned this way and that in front of the glass, just staring at her own reflection. "I look—" she finally said.

"Lovely," I finished for her. The buttery yellow just suited her, bringing out the blue of her eyes and the sheen of her hair. "You have to agree to come to the masquerade now, Anne. You can't possibly let this dress go to waste, lying in a trunk up here."

Anne looked at her reflection another moment. Then she nodded with sudden decision. "All right," she said. "I will come." And then she smiled and looked down at her feet, nearly hidden by the skirts of the gown. "You'll have to help me hem this, though. I'm uncertain enough of my dancing without worrying the entire evening that I'm going to trip on my own costume."

I did help her hem it. The waist had to be taken in just a little, as well, so we brought the gown down to my room to make the alterations. We have been working all afternoon, except that I ducked downstairs to where Mr. Folliet was playing billiards—or rather practising on his own in the game room—and enlisted his help in getting Mr. Carter to the masquerade as well. Properly masked and attired, Mr. Folliet promised me. And at my request he said that he would invite Caroline, as well.

But apart from that, I have been upstairs with Anne all day. The alterations to the yellow gown took us until just an hour ago—hence the relative simplicity of my own costume—because I was terrified of spoiling the silk with uneven stitches. And I did not dare call in any of the maids to help us; I was worried that if any of the servants knew, word would get back to Aunt de Bourgh, and my aunt would bully Anne into giving up on going to the masquerade after all.

Now, though, the hemming is finished, my bonnet is trimmed with a length of the yellow silk and a bunch of pink silk flowers, besides, and I have sent Anne off to her own room to dress. I helped her to curl her hair, and I have even persuaded her to wear a pair of my silk stockings instead of her usual woollen ones. We are to meet Mr. Folliet and Mr. Carter downstairs in twenty minutes time. I only hope—

I had to stop writing just now. Someone knocked at my door—and my heart tried to jump up into my throat at the sound, for fear it was Aunt de Bourgh. But it was only Elizabeth. She had come, she said, to ask whether I would slap my brother's cheeks if he tried to apologise again.

"I would never—" I began, shocked, and Elizabeth laughed.

"No, I know you wouldn't, Georgiana. You're too sweet-tempered by half, as I said before. But—" she studied my face. "Your brother really does wish to apologise again. Will you forgive him? He would have come himself, but he didn't wish to upset you any more."

"Did you know of Wickham's attempts at blackmail?" I asked her.

Elizabeth shook her head. "No. I . . . I did suspect that something was troubling your brother. But no more than that." She paused and then said, "Your brother is very reserved. Though he *is* your own brother, so I'm surely telling you nothing you do not already know as well as I. You and he are very much alike, really. Of course, I'm sure you know that already, as well. He is"—Elizabeth smiled a little—"learning to share his worries. But I don't like to push him too much, either.

Even a married man deserves his privacy, surely. So, no. I didn't know about Wickham's letter to him. If I had, I would have told Darcy that in my opinion, you ought to be informed of the matter. But—"she trailed off, then said, a flicker of worry in her dark eyes, "*are* you still angry with him, Georgiana? I hope you'll speak to him yourself and accept his apology." Elizabeth smiled again. "I never had a brother. Though I should have liked one. But I think it's likely difficult for any elder brother to accept that his younger sister has all of a sudden grown up."

"I know. And I am not angry with him," I told her. I truly was not. There was a strange burning, scraping feeling inside my chest. There is yet. But it wasn't—isn't—directed at my brother. At least I do not think it is.

Am I still angry with myself? Maybe. I suppose I must be. Or Edward?

But I had better finish writing this, or it will be time for me to leave before I've done.

Elizabeth let out a breath of relief. "I'm so glad." And then she seemed to take in my velvet cloak and crown of flowers for the first time. "But why are you wearing fancy dress?" she asked.

I explained about Anne and the masquerade ball—and when I had finished, Elizabeth clapped her hands over her mouth to keep from laughing. The worry had gone from her eyes. "You've actually managed to persuade Anne to attend a masquerade? You must be either a miracle worker or a witch," she said. "But how are you planning to get her out of the house?"

"That's just it," I admitted. "I'm afraid if Anne sees her mother before we leave, she won't have the courage to go at all. My aunt will realise Anne is missing when she's not here for dinner, of course. But by then it will be too late for her to do anything. It's only keeping Aunt de Bourgh from seeing us get into the carriage that's the real trouble."

"Never mind." A touch of mischief crept into Elizabeth's smile. "I believe I am about to have an urgent need for Lady Catherine's opinion on some new shelves I was thinking of having installed in one of the closets. In a room far, far at the back of the house."

"Oh, thank you!" I did not doubt that would keep my aunt occupied. "And please, will you tell my brother I'm not angry and will see him tomorrow? I imagine you will have retired for the night by the time we've returned."

"Of course I'll tell him." Elizabeth hugged me. "And I hope you have a splendid, wonderful time at the ball."

And now the little clock on my mantle is showing the hour, so I had better stop writing and go down to meet the others. Elizabeth has gone already to distract my aunt, so I hope we will indeed be able to get Anne away in secret.

All that remains is to see what kind of a time we have at the masquerade.

Monday 23 May 1814

I had not thought I would be picking up this diary again tonight, directly we returned from the ball. But I can't sleep. And neither can I face the thought of lying in bed and staring up at the ceiling, counting the minutes as they slip by.

So I am writing instead, curled up on the window seat. I suppose Mrs. Reynolds will be appalled when she sees how many candles I have gone through these last weeks.

In fact, I only need one word to answer my earlier question of what sort of time we had at the ball: Horrible.

No, actually, that is not fair. Anne and Mr. Carter certainly enjoyed themselves. Mr. Folliet may have, too, save for being punched in the jaw.

Thanks to Elizabeth, we did manage to leave the house without being seen by Aunt de Bourgh. Anne was nervous and kept tugging at the strings of her (my) bonnet. But she looked truly exquisite—she really did—in the yellow gown, with colour in her cheeks and golden curls framing her face.

Mr. Folliet met us in the hall. He had asked Mrs. Reynolds for help with a costume, he told me. And she had found him a grenadier's uniform that once belonged to her uncle, who fought in the war with the American colonies. The red coat, with its blue velvet facing on the lapels and gleaming brass buttons, did smell rather of the moth balls Mrs. Reynolds keeps it in—but it fit Mr. Folliet beautifully. And he wore a powdered wig and a black three-cornered hat, as well, to complete the costume.

Caroline was feeling ill and had declined coming. But true to his word, Mr. Folliet had somehow persuaded Mr. Carter to attend. And had got him into a costume, too, of a kind: a black friar's robe, with a rope belt and a heavy wooden cross worn around his neck.

When he saw Anne, Mr. Carter's jaw did not drop open and he did not stare, exactly. He just went very still. And then he crossed to Anne and took her hand and said, without even stammering, "You look beautiful, Miss de Bourgh."

The assembly rooms had been decorated for the
dance, all draped in garlands of flowers. There were ice
sculptures on the supper tables, and the candles in the
chandeliers overhead shone.

There were crowds of people already there when we
arrived, all masked and costumed as we were. Har-
lequins and Columbines. Gypsy maidens. Crusader
knights and Egyptian queens and Red Riding Hoods.

There was dancing, of course. When we arrived, the
musicians had already begun to play. At first I was
nervous for Anne's sake—I could not help but watch
her, afraid that she would trip or have some mischance
during one of the figures. But she did amazingly well.
Mr. Folliet partnered her for the first two dances, and
led her through just as they'd been practising and I
think that bolstered her confidence. I rather lost track
of her after that, but every time I caught a glimpse of her
she was smiling or laughing. And I did see her dance
with Mr. Carter at least three times. And she went into
the supper room with him, besides.

That was when it happened. I was dancing with
Mr. Folliet and had just seen Anne and Mr. Carter go in
to supper when I suddenly began to feel faint.

I suppose it served me right for pretending to feel
dizzy with Edward the night of the Herrons' party. I
had lied about faintness then, so I was struck with it in
truth now. For the first time in my life, too; I never faint
as a rule.

But—I suddenly realised as my vision tilted and the
room began to swim about me—between George Wickham's appearance before breakfast and then working
on Anne's costume all the afternoon, I had entirely forgotten to have anything to eat all day.

Mr. Folliet was everything attentive and kind. I could not face the thought of all the noise and crowd in the supper room, so he brought me downstairs to the level of the street and out into the open air.

The coachmen and other servants were having their own supper and party in the yard outside the assembly rooms. Some of the laughter and singing floated out towards us, but apart from that, the street was quiet. There was a bench, between two of the trees that lined the road on either side, and Mr. Folliet led me there.

My head cleared and I felt very much better once I had sat down, and once I had assured Mr. Folliet that I was not ill, only thirsty and hungry, he went and fetched us both plates from the supper room. Roast chicken and cold ham and pickles and gooseberry fool.

"In short," Mr. Folliet said, "an array of every dish that looked as though I could carry it without staining Mrs. Reynolds's uncle's coat. I promised her I'd have it back to her in pristine condition at the end of the night."

He spoke with a flash of his usual smile. But he was quiet all the time we were eating. Our bench was a little distance away from the lanterns that lighted the doors to the assembly room, so the shadows were too thick to see his face clearly. But I could feel him watching me. And then when we had both finished, he seemed to hesitate, then said, "Miss Darcy, may I ask you something?"

I felt a qualm about my heart at that, for fear he was going to propose. I do like him very much. But I don't love him at all.

Of course, my aunt would say that is no reason whatsoever to refuse a man's proposal. Marriage has little or nothing to do with love.

Maybe at one time I even might have been persuaded—

not exactly to agree, but at least to accept a marriage based on liking or respect rather than love. But not after seeing Elizabeth and my brother together. I may sometimes feel lonely, seeing the two of them so happy in each other. But it would be lonelier still to know that I had lost my chance at that kind of happiness forever by marrying a man I did not love.

All that flashed through my mind in an instant—the fear that Mr. Folliet might propose, the sickness that swept through me at the thought of having to decline. I felt much worse just at the thought of it than I did actually refusing Sir John. Because I *do* like Mr. Folliet so much.

If he was planning to propose, though, he never got the chance. I'd barely nodded in answer to his question when all at once he was yanked to his feet and then sent reeling backwards by a hard punch full in the face.

"I thought I told you to stay away from her, you little swine!"

It was Edward's voice, low and rough with anger, and Edward's lean, broad-shouldered form that appeared out of the shadows to strike Mr. Folliet on the jaw. But the whole was so unbelievable that I thought for a moment that this was some fresh hallucination from going all day without food.

I roused myself to jump up, though, and caught hold of Edward's arm before he could strike Mr. Folliet again. "Edward, stop it!" I cried. "What in the world do you think you're doing?"

"You know his character, Georgiana." It was too dark to see much of Edward's face, either. But his voice sounded as though he bit the words off from between clenched teeth, and the muscles of his arm were iron hard, taut and quivering under my grip. "Or you ought to, by now. What on earth possessed you to meet him out here—"

I was still so stunned that my thoughts felt like the jolting movements of a clockwork toy. But still, realisation dawned. In the dark, all that Edward—or anyone— would be able to distinguish of the uniform was the red coat. The same shade of red still used on the uniforms of the army regulars.

The same thought had evidently struck Mr. Folliet. Or part of the same thought, at least, for so far as I know, he knows nothing about George Wickham. His lower lip was bleeding from Edward's blow; he had been thrown backwards, closer to the lighted lantern posts, and I could see the trickle of blood on his jaw.

He had one hand clamped over his mouth, muffling his words, but he said—very politely, considering that he had just been punched by a bare acquaintance and entirely without provocation—"Is it possible you may have mistaken me for someone else?"

Edward stared at him. His mouth dropped open and his throat worked as though he were trying to speak, but no words emerged. I might have found it comical under any other circumstances. But as it was, I was far too furious.

"You actually thought I would be idiot enough to meet with George Wickham, alone and at night?" I demanded. "And what are you doing here, Edward? Were you following me?"

I heard Edward draw one hissing breath through his teeth, then another. He didn't look at me, but said, to Mr. Folliet, "My most sincere apologies, sir. I did indeed mistake you for someone else. If there's anything I can do—"

Mr. Folliet had found a handkerchief and pressed it to his bleeding lip, but he waved the apology away with his free hand. "Nothing, save perhaps explain to Mrs. Reynolds for me why there is blood on her uncle's coat. I don't think I can stand being struck in the face twice in the same night."

The rigid line of Edward's shoulders relaxed. "Done. Though I will let you in on the secret that Mrs. Reynolds's bark is a good deal worse than her bite." He put out his hand. "I really do apologise, Mr. Folliet. Though that sounds very inadequate, I know." He let out a ragged breath and raked a hand through his hair. "I feel as though I ought to let you strike me in the face in return."

Mr. Folliet accepted the hand Edward offered and they shook. "Nothing so drastic is necessary, I assure you. Besides"—Mr. Folliet was looking at me—"I rather imagine the score may be evened on my behalf, and sooner than you think, if Miss Darcy here has anything to say."

He stepped back before Edward could respond. "And now I ought to leave you and go in search of some cold water to use on these bloodstains. Mrs. Reynolds may accept my apology more readily if I can assure her that I did everything possible to keep the stains from becoming set."

He vanished inside, and Edward turned to me. "Georgiana, I—"

I interrupted. Mr. Folliet was perfectly right. Just then I *was* feeling angry enough to strike Edward across the face. "You *were* following me. And you actually had so low an opinion of my good sense as to believe that I would come out here with George Wickham alone.

As though I would be naive enough ever to trust him again—especially after the threats he made to my brother!"

Edward passed a hand across his forehead. "I heard from Elizabeth that you had come here, to a public assembly. I was . . . concerned that Wickham would try to approach you again. So I decided to come after you, yes. And as for your other charge—you were fond of Wickham, at one time."

I could hear him struggling to speak patiently—which only made me angrier still. I felt as though acid were eating outwards from the hot, clenched space in my chest. "Yes, perhaps—before I knew his true character! But I'm not a child anymore to be won over by an amiable word and a charming smile—however much you and my brother persist in treating me as one!"

Dark as it was, I saw Edward's jaw clench. "And yet I did find you out here, unchaperoned, and in the company of an unmarried man. You seem, still, to have small care for the harm such behaviour may do your reputation."

"We were in full view of three dozen serving women and coachmen!" I gestured across to where the servants' party was still going on in the carriage yard. "On a public street. And Mr. Folliet behaved as a perfect gentleman."

"That's not the point." Edward's voice still sounded tight and stiff. "If word of this got round, people might still say—"

"Oh, yes, people might certainly talk!" All of a sudden, the hot, tight space inside my chest had cracked wide open. I hadn't even realised how angry I was until I felt the words spilling out. "Because I'm a woman. If I were a man, I might visit every house of ill-repute in

London, keep a dozen or more mistresses on a string—and the world would slap me on the back and cheer me on. It's true, isn't it?" I took a step towards Edward. "Can you look me in the eyes and tell me that *you* have never—"

"Georgiana!" Edward rubbed a hand across the back of his neck and then went on in a quieter tone. "Good God, how do you even—"

"Know of such things? I told you, I'm not a child. I have lived in London ever since I left school; I know what goes on. And I know that merely because I'm a woman, the merest whisper of a rumour that I might *almost* have eloped with the son of my father's steward and my reputation would be forever ruined. No gentleman—not even one of those who *does* keep a dozen mistresses and spends his nights in the brothels, besides—would consent to have me for a wife."

"I never claimed that it was fair. Only that it is true." Edward cleared his throat, then went on in the same quiet tone. "And as your guardian, Georgiana, I am responsible for pointing out the way of the world, however unjust it may be." He cleared his throat again. "Are you—that is, are you and Mr. Folliet likely to become engaged?"

His face was an austere mask in the shadows; lantern light gleamed like metal on the lines of his temple and jaw. His voice, too, was all but expressionless, impersonal and polite.

And all at once my throat ached and for the second time today I felt my eyes stinging. "I am sure that as my guardian, you would greatly prefer it if I were. You would be spared all worry of what damage tonight might do my reputation. And be spared having to ride out after George Wickham again, besides."

I managed to get the words out without my voice shaking. But I could not trust myself anymore. I turned and ran back inside the door to the assembly rooms. I heard Edward calling after me, but I did not stop. And Edward did not follow me inside.

Tuesday 24 May 1814

Elizabeth is going to have a baby!

I am so happy for her. Her and my brother, both.

It was completely by accident that I found out. Well, accident and eavesdropping. Though I truly did not mean to overhear.

Despite going to bed so late last night, I woke early and could not fall back to sleep. And I was afraid that if I stayed in the house, I might meet with Edward.

So I went out for a walk before breakfast—and happened on M. de La Courcelle, of all people, walking in the garden with Aunt de Bourgh. I suppose he must have come to see Caroline and met my aunt as he approached the house. At least for Caroline's sake I *hope* he came here to see her.

I have been wondering whether there has been some quarrel or trouble between them, because Caroline has been looking even paler than Elizabeth these last few days. It is not just her declining to come to the ball last night. And unlike Elizabeth, she seems no better in the afternoons and evenings.

At any rate, M. de La Courcelle must have offered Aunt de Bourgh his arm, because her hand rested on his bent elbow. They were strolling together past the lilac bushes that grow by the south wing of the house, and as they came near, I heard M. de La Courcelle say, "Ah, but this scent, it reminds me always of my *grand-mère* the *duchesse.* She grew lilacs always at her chateaux in Aix."

They hadn't seen me yet; I was partially screened by the bushes. And all at once, I absolutely couldn't face the thought of M. de La Courcelle's hand-kissing. Or my aunt's anger.

I am not such a fool as to think I can indefinitely postpone the inevitable tirade of reproaches for bringing Anne to the masquerade. And maybe I'm gaining courage—or at least not such a coward as I used to be—because I do not seem to dread it as much as I might once have done. But all the same, this morning, every word of Edward's polite, *As your guardian, I am responsible for pointing out the way of the world*, speech felt as though they were still being driven into my ears like spikes. And I just couldn't stand the thought of meeting M. de La Courcelle and Aunt de Bourgh, as well.

I stepped quickly backwards, towards the house, and then blindly ducked through the first open door I came to. It was the French door in Elizabeth's own little parlour, as it happened, where she sits to write letters or sew on her own. I had come up behind the heavy length of velvet curtain that keeps drafts from the door out of the room—and I was just about to push the draperies aside when I heard voices and realised Elizabeth and Fitzwilliam were alone together. Or had been until I'd come.

It was the tone of their voices that made me stop and stand, frozen.

"A baby?" my brother said. He sounded stunned. "Truly?"

"It has been known to happen." Elizabeth was laughing, but there was a little quaver as of tears, as well. "Are you happy about it, then? I didn't want to tell you until I was sure."

And my brother said, "Happy?" There was a soft rustle of fabric, and I knew he'd pulled her close to him. "Do you have the faintest idea how much I love you?"

The laughter was entirely gone from Elizabeth's voice as she whispered, "Oh, but I do."

I stepped back as softly and slowly as I possibly could, back out into the garden and pulled the door closed behind me. And then—counting the doors, this time—I found the music room and went inside.

Elizabeth found me there a little while later. Her cheeks were still flushed and her eyes were bright—and she had come to tell me properly, so really it did not make so much difference that I had overheard.

"Aunt Georgiana," Elizabeth said when she had given me the news—and I must have pretended surprise enough, because she did not seem to notice anything amiss.

"Yes, Aunt Georgiana," I repeated. "It sounds terribly old and proper, doesn't it? I'll have to make sure my behaviour sets a proper auntly example from here on. Maybe Aunt de Bourgh can give me lessons."

And Elizabeth laughed and said, "Don't even think it! And actually I've far more confidence in the thought of you as an aunt than me as a mother. I'm afraid I'm not nearly sober or serious enough for the responsibility."

"You needn't worry," I told her. "My own mother was never sober or serious—I loved that in her."

Elizabeth's smile faded and she put her hand on my arm. "Georgiana, I—" But I shook my head. "No, don't spoil such a happy day." I hugged her. "I am so very glad for you, Elizabeth."

I truly am.

I think I'll go find Anne and drag her out with me to visit the village poor again. Before I bump into Edward in the hall or the library or the drawing room.

I have not seen him yet today, but I cannot hope to avoid him forever—the house isn't *that* large.

Later . . .

I have an hour before dinner to write this. I feel so sick with guilt, I think I have to.

I did persuade Anne to come out with me this afternoon. Actually, it did not take any persuading on my part at all. She came quite readily. And she even brought several shillings in her reticule on purpose to give to old Mrs. Tate for the hawthorn berry tonic Mrs. Tate had promised her.

Mrs. Tate tried to give some of the money back, saying that it was too much, but Anne would not hear of it. "Oh, but this is just payment in advance on any future bottles you make for me," she said. She held up the bottle of murky-grey liquid Mrs. Tate had given her and said, without even a tremor of irony in her voice, "I have no doubt I'll be wanting more."

Mrs. Tate was so pleased. She's promised Anne that she will have her *glowin' like a rose in full bloom* before a month has gone by.

Anne thanked her—and waited until we were well out of sight of Mrs. Tate's cottage before she emptied the tonic bottle into a bush.

She asked whether she ought to take some first—just so that she could tell Mrs. Tate she had tried the tonic without telling a lie.

"Not unless you're tired of living—or at the very least, hoping to spend the rest of the day in bed with stomach pains," I told her. And we both laughed.

And then, quite suddenly, Anne started to cry. It was not at all like when I found her sobbing in the music room. She cried very quietly, this time, without any noise. Just the tears rolling down her cheeks under the brim of her bonnet.

"Anne, what is it?" I asked her.

We were walking up the lane to where we'd left Jem and the barouche. There was rain a few nights ago, and the road to Mrs. Tate's had been too deep in mud for Jem to risk the wheels getting stuck.

Anne wiped the tears away with the back of her gloved hand. "What is it?" She let out a sound that was half ragged breath, half choking laugh. "It's Mr. Carter, that's what it is."

"Mr. Carter? But didn't you have an agreeable time with him at the masquerade last night? I thought that you'd—"

"I did." Anne swallowed and brushed at her eyes again. "It was lovely. It was"—her voice was suddenly almost fierce—"it was the loveliest night I have ever had in my entire life. That is just the trouble." She looked up at me. "Can you see my mother ever in a thousand years agreeing to my marrying Mr. Carter?"

That brought me up so sharply it was like a slap in the face. I had been so entirely focused on drawing Anne out of her shell—and so pleased that Mr. Carter seemed truly to like her—that I had not thought through to what the ending was likely to be. Anne was perfectly right. Aunt de Bourgh would never consent to her daughter's marrying a penniless clergyman. To be perfectly fair to my aunt, it's not just her—I doubt many earls' daughters would let their own daughters marry men in Mr. Carter's situation in life.

"I do have my own money," Anne went on. "My father left it to me. But I can't have it until I marry—and only then if my mother gives her consent to the match." Her lips twisted bitterly. "You can well imagine my mother insisted that my father include *that* clause in his will."

I said, "You're of age. You could marry Mr. Carter without your mother's consent. So long as you were willing to be poor."

Anne heard the doubt in my voice. She gave me a brief, fractured twist of a smile. "You may not believe me, Georgiana, but I *would* be willing to be poor, actually. It's not so simple as that, though. John—Mr. Carter—has no parish of his own. He's only holding his present vicarage—it's one within the gift of Sir Hugh Annesley, in Kent—until Sir Hugh's second son is old enough to take it. Which the boy will be next year. And then John will have no living at all, nor even anywhere to live. And if I married him, don't you think my mother would use every scrap of influence she had to ensure that no one ever *would* invest him with his own vicarage?"

"Surely not," I said. "You're her own daughter. She might be angry at first, but she'd—"

"She doesn't love me, you know." Anne's voice was clogged with crying but quite matter-of-fact. "I'm a great disappointment to her. I think she would have liked a daughter who was spirited and bold. Like your brother's wife Elizabeth, actually. But I'm not and never have been—and she punishes me by telling me I'm ill all the time. If I disappointed her in who I married, too, she'd be far too angry to ever forgive me. She would sooner see me starve than wedded to a man she disapproved of." Anne brushed at her cheeks. "If I married Mr. Carter, I'd ruin his life. I'm not going to do that to him."

"Does Mr. Carter . . . does he care for you, too?"

"I think so." Anne swallowed. "He said—or at least hinted—as much. But he said he was in no position to make any declarations of love. That is how I know of his situation with regards his vicarage. He was very . . . very honourable. He told me that with nothing, not even a home, to offer a wife, he couldn't insult any woman he truly cared for by telling her how he felt. "

Anne wasn't crying anymore, only staring straight ahead, her eyes fixed and unblinking. "So he'll leave Pemberley in another two weeks' time. And I'll go back to Rosings with my mother. And I'll never see him again."

That is why I feel so sick with guilt now. I meant to help Anne—but I have succeeded only in making life worse than ever for her.

Mr. Carter is probably the first man who has ever really talked to Anne. It's no wonder she fell in love with him. I remember how I felt about George Wickham.

But if it had not been for me, Anne never would have begun to care for Mr. Carter. Or maybe she would, a little, but only in so far as to admire him from a distance. She wouldn't have spoken to him or danced with him— or heard him make guarded, doomed declarations of love.

It must be far worse, I think, to lose all hope of freedom when you have been given just a taste. If it weren't for me, Anne would never really have known what she was missing in living so constantly under her mother's thumb.

It is my fault that she is so unhappy now. And I can't see any way of setting matters straight again.

Later still . . .

I seem to keep putting this diary down and then picking it back up again today. But I forgot to say that I spoke to my brother, in between coming back from my outing with Anne and going upstairs to dress for dinner.

He apologised—again—for keeping Wickham's demands from me. And I told him I had long since forgiven him—and hugged him and said how happy I was about Elizabeth's and his expectations.

And then I told him that I wanted him to promise me that he would not pay Wickham anything more. That it was my error, and that it was intolerable that he should be the one who had to pay for it.

"*Your* error?" Fitzwilliam shook his head. The line of his mouth had tightened. "Mine, rather. I should have protected you from him. I could have made his true character known to you much earlier. And I should certainly not have left you in the charge of Mrs. Younge."

"When I was ten, you were left to be father and mother to me, both," I told him. "And without warning. You can't blame yourself for having been unprepared for the role. And you'll have to learn to let children make their own mistakes, or your future son or daughter will turn your hair snow white before you're five-and-thirty."

Fitzwilliam smiled at that.

"But I'm not ten any longer," I said. "Nor yet fifteen, to be alternately dazzled and frightened into an elopement. I do know my own mind—and I have thought long and hard about my decision. I truly do not wish you to pay Wickham one single farthing more. Let him spread what rumours of me he likes. I won't have us living our whole lives afraid of him, constantly bowing to his demands. For if you pay him now, you can't imagine he won't be back for more, when he's run through his current funds."

My brother looked at me, long and hard. I could see him wishing to refuse and forcing himself not to. At last he said, "You do realise the damage that may be done by Wickham's speaking out?"

"You mean that my reputation will be blemished," I said. "I do know it. But not—at least I hope not—in the eyes of anyone who truly knows my character. And as for marriage—I wouldn't *want* to marry any man who was frightened off by mere rumour, from the mouth of someone like George Wickham. I would not wish to marry anyone who would not at least give me the chance to explain the truth of what happened at Ramsgate."

I could see my brother stopping himself from interrupting again, and I pressed forward. "If you heard anything to Elizabeth's discredit—wouldn't you ask her yourself without letting it alter your opinion of her in the slightest? I know how much you love her—how could I not, living with the two of you for this past year? Can you suppose I would wish to marry a man who did not feel the same about me?"

My brother let out his breath. Slowly, he nodded his head. "It's hard for me to agree to what you ask. Hard for me not to wish to shield you from the consequences of what I still blame myself for. But if that's truly what you wish—"

"It is." I felt my chest expand with the force of the relief that filled me. I took a breath, then asked, "And will you tell me what's become of Wickham now?"

Fitzwilliam seemed to hesitate. But then he said, "Edward found Wickham in the garden where you'd left him. He didn't tell me exactly what had passed between them, but"—a grim smile touched the edges of my brother's mouth. "But I rather think Edward gave Wickham a lesson in good manners that he won't forget in a hurry. And that, I think, will make him hesitate to intrude on the grounds of Pemberley again."

I didn't—I still don't—entirely like the idea of Edward's thrashing Wickham for my sake. As though I were the helpless princess in a children's fairy tale, who cannot take care of herself without the prince riding to her rescue.

But I have to admit that I am relieved, too, if Edward has truly frightened Wickham off, because it means I need not face him again.

Fitzwilliam paused, then said, with studied casualness, "You've been in the company of Mr. Folliet a good deal of late."

"Oh, not you, too!" I told him. "I've heard the same from Elizabeth—and Edward, as well!"

My brother laughed. "I'm still your elder brother. It's my job to keep a stern eye on all possible suitors for your hand."

"I like Mr. Folliet—I like him very much. But I'm not . . . I mean, I don't—"

"All right." My brother held up his hands. "I'll spare you any further interrogation. Just promise me that if you do decide in favour of someone, you'll tell me about it?"

"I promise." I hugged him again.

"And don't be too angry with Edward for what happened last night," my brother added. "He meant for the best."

My head jerked up. "Edward told you? That he'd—"

"Punched poor Folliet in the face? He did. He came home and demanded strong drink to help rid him of the memory," my brother said.

I don't know why it should bother me that Edward repeated everything of last night's events to my brother. But there's still a prickling feeling like anger running to the tips of my fingers at the thought.

Is it the thought of Edward coming home to discuss me with my brother? As though I truly were the helpless princess in a tower—or a little girl?

I'm not sure.

I managed not to see Edward at all today, except at dinner, where the only words I had to speak to him were "thank you" when he passed me the salt.

Thursday 26 May 1814

I can truly say that I have never, ever been more surprised or shocked in my entire life. There is really no way of working up to this, so I will just write it straight out:

Aunt de Bourgh is engaged to be married to M. de La Courcelle.

Even seeing it here, in ink on my page, I can scarcely believe it. I'm sitting here in the window seat of the morning room, half-expecting the letters to dissolve and rearrange themselves on the page into some other words entirely.

But it is true. We had just finished with breakfast when M. de La Courcelle's arrival was announced. He came into the room, and Aunt de Bourgh rose to meet him, gave him her hand, and then turned to us all and said she had an announcement to make: she and M. de

La Courcelle were going to be married.

There was a moment of absolute, stunned silence from all of us sitting around the table.

M. de La Courcelle appeared to notice nothing amiss, though. He only pressed Aunt de Bourgh's hand to his lips and said that she did him more honour than he could say, and that truly, today he was the happiest of men.

My brother was the first to recover himself. He rose from his place at the head of the table and went to kiss Aunt de Bourgh's cheek and offer his congratulations. There was a stiffness in his manner, I think, when he turned to offer M. de La Courcelle his hand. But he did shake with him. And he responded perfectly politely when M. de La Courcelle put his hand over his heart and promised "on my life, to cherish your beloved aunt as she so richly deserves."

I was watching M. de La Courcelle, because I was so very surprised after the attentions he had paid to Caroline. I kept searching for a look of consciousness, a flicker of guilt or regret or *something*. There was nothing to be seen, though. M. de La Courcelle looked just as always: handsome, suave, very polished and self-assured. His snowy-white neck cloth falling in precise folds over his chest. His boots polished to a mirror sheen. His dark hair curling over his aristocratic brow.

And my aunt looked?

I can't entirely put into words how Aunt de Bourgh looked. Happy? Perhaps she was. I mean, whatever I may think of the match, I *do* hope she is happy in her engagement to M. de La Courcelle.

Maybe it is only because I cannot remember ever seeing my aunt really happy that triumphant seems a better word to describe how she looked. Triumphant and proud as she stood there, her arm resting on M. de La Courcelle's arm.

The two of them went out shortly after, in my aunt's carriage. They were to drive into Lambton, so Aunt de Bourgh said, to dispatch a notice to the *Times*, so that an announcement of the engagement might be made in next week's papers.

Caroline stumbled up from her place at table and rushed blindly out of the room almost the instant M. de La Courcelle and my aunt were gone. Poor Caroline. However much I may have resented her in the past, I am so sorry for her now.

To lose my brother to Elizabeth was bad enough. But to lose M. de La Courcelle to Aunt de Bourgh—

Caroline sat as though frozen, just staring at them all the while Aunt de Bourgh was making her announcement. But I was sitting next to her, and so saw how tightly her hands were clenched in her lap, and that her whole body was shivering as though she were using all her will not to move or cry out.

Anne looked every bit as stunned as I felt. Not upset or unhappy, I don't think—just utterly surprised. She turned to Mr. Carter, who was sitting beside her, and said, "John—" and Mr. Carter murmured something I did not hear and took her hands and led her out.

Mr. Folliet rose, too, and bowed and said something about realising that our family might like time to speak together alone, without the presence of outsiders. Which was very perceptive and thoughtful of him. My brother nodded and thanked him. And when Mr. Folliet had gone, it was only Fitzwilliam, Elizabeth, Edward, and me left in the breakfast room.

Edward was the first to speak. "He's a bloody French fortune hunter," he said. "He has to be."

No one contradicted him. It is terrible to say, perhaps, but I do not think any of us imagined for a moment that M. de La Courcelle might truly care for Aunt de Bourgh.

My brother rubbed the place between his eyes as though it ached. "Of course he is. And there's no mystery about why he should want to marry Aunt de Bourgh. As wealthy as she is, and as great an estate as she has? What confounds my mind is how she can possibly have been taken in by a smooth, oily, sycophantic little swine like him."

Elizabeth's mouth curved just a little at that. "So, then, what do you *really* think of him?" Her brief smile faded, though, and she put a hand on my brother's arm. "You're not thinking. To whom did your aunt last bestow her patronage? Mr. Collins—as toadying and sycophantic a man as ever opened his mouth. Simply because he knew how best to flatter and fawn on her. Lady Catherine de Bourgh has spent the whole of her life frightening and intimidating people and making them resent and fear her. What does she know of true, sincere love? I doubt anyone has ever loved her in her life. Setting yourself up as Queen of the Castle—as your aunt has done—doesn't just make one proud and unreasonable and tyrannical. It makes one terribly vulnerable, as well."

There was a moment's silence, and then Edward said, turning to my brother, "Is there anything to be done, do you think?"

My brother's brows drew together, but he slowly shook his head. "I don't believe so. What can we do? We could try to discover more about M. de La Courcelle. But the war in France makes such inquiries next to impossible. And besides, even if we learned anything to the man's discredit, what good would it do? Would

Aunt de Bourgh listen to either of us? I doubt it. If she's already gone to post an announcement to the Times, she won't turn back now—whatever we learned about M. de La Courcelle. Breaking the engagement would mean admitting publicly that she'd made a mistake. She'd never bring herself to do that."

I had to leave off writing just now. Mr. Folliet came into the morning room to ask whether there was anything he could do to be of assistance. He even offered to move to the Lambton Inn—or leave the neighbourhood entirely, if our family wished to be alone at this time.

But I told him of course he need not go. As my brother said, what is done is done. And Aunt de Bourgh should be free to marry whomever she chooses.

Mr. Folliet studied me a moment, then sat down on the window seat beside me. "You know," he said, "I'd a great uncle—my grandfather's brother—who reached the age of seventy, still a crusted and cantankerous old bachelor. And then suddenly announced he was going to marry his housekeeper, a woman of five-and-thirty."

"And what happened?" I asked.

Mr. Folliet shrugged. "His heirs were furious, of course, because the old boy was immensely rich and the thought of all that inheritance going to a servant instead of to them . . . "

"Were you angry, as well?" I asked.

"Me?" Mr. Folliet looked surprised. "I've enough of an income to satisfy my wants—I don't begrudge my uncle's housekeeper a chance at what must have seemed an impossibly large fortune to her. And you know, they were quite happy together, after a fashion. Mrs. Hastings—that was the woman's name—took very good care of my uncle. Nursed him devotedly during his last illness. And she proved to have a surprisingly good head for business—she's done a fine job of managing his estates ever since he died."

I know what Mr. Folliet meant to imply—that my aunt's marriage to M. de La Courcelle may turn out all right after all. It was very good of him.

Mr. Folliet is gone—he had some letters to write, so he said.

I'd meant to go into the music room and practice the pianoforte. But even knowing that what Mr. Folliet said may be true, I don't think I could pay attention to the music just now.

Maybe I will take my sketching pad and pencils out into the grounds instead.

Later . . .

It's evening now. I'm in my room—I shall have to dress for dinner soon. My brother has of course invited M. de La Courcelle to join us for the meal.

I did go out into the garden this morning. Though at the moment I wish I had spent the entire morning with Aunt de Bourgh and M. de La Courcelle. Or darning stockings. Or helping the stable hands muck out the horses' stalls.

Anything, in fact, except what I actually did do—which was take my sketch pad and a folding chair out onto the slope of lawn behind the house.

I had just settled myself in the shade of one of the big Spanish oaks when I looked up to see Edward walking towards me.

I expected him to pass on—we have scarcely spoken since we as good as quarrelled the night of the masquerade ball. But he stopped beside me. He did not speak, though—not at first. If I had not believed the word could never be used to describe Edward, I would have said he looked uncertain as he asked at last, "Would you . . . would you object strongly to company?"

"That depends on the company," I said. "If it's yours, I shouldn't object at all. If it's anyone else's—M. de La Courcelle's, for example—"

Edward laughed and dropped down on the lawn beside my chair. He'd taken off his coat and cravat. He was wearing breaches and a cream-coloured shirt. He must have been walking for some time; sweat darkened his collar and streaked his bare throat. He leaned back on his elbows, stretching his long legs out before him on the grass.

"It's not even the difference in their ages that I mind," he said. "I've always thought of her as ancient—but I suppose Aunt de Bourgh is only about fifteen years M. de La Courcelle's elder. And of course their marriage doesn't affect me in the least. I mean to say"—Edward frowned, looking back towards the house, his eyes narrowed against the sun—"I may have a strong urge to kick Courcelle down the stairs every time he starts spouting his flowery compliments. But it's not as though I'm the one who'll have to live with the man. It's more—" Edward's shoulders shifted under the fabric of his shirt. I could see the outline of the bandage around his upper arm, but the wound didn't seem to pain him any longer. "I don't know," he said at last. "It's always unsettling, I suppose, to realise how little you really know of anyone else. I've known Aunt de Bourgh since I was a boy—and if you'd told me even up until yesterday that she would marry again—and M. de La Courcelle, of all the men in England—I'd have said you'd taken leave of your senses."

"I know," I said. Because that was it exactly, the feeling I could not put into words before. "Remember what you said about Pemberley? That you felt as though nothing changes here. It's all safe and constant. But I would have said Aunt de Bourgh was just as utterly fixed and unchangeable. I'm not . . . I've never been fond of her. But she's a constant—or she has been. Now this. She's not as fierce or as frightening as I thought. She's not even the woman I believed her to be, if she can be taken in by M. de La Courcelle. I feel just as I did when the old elm tree was uprooted in the storm last summer. As though something ancient and invulnerable had fallen down."

Edward was silent a moment. He had pulled a blade of grass and was turning it between his teeth. Then he tilted his head to look up at me. Sunlight slanting through the leaves above us dappled his lean face and dark hair as his eyes met mine. "I never said that I *believed* things couldn't change here. Only that Pemberley has the ability to cast that illusion. But it is an illusion. Everything changes in this world. Including ourselves."

The shadow I had seen before was back in his eyes, the edge of tension or sadness or worry hardening the planes of his face and tightening his jaw.

I was unsure what to say—or whether I should even say anything at all. But he looked all at once so different from the Edward I had grown up with—and above all so very alone—that I asked after a moment's hesitation, "Are you thinking of . . . the war?"

Edward didn't answer, only sat staring down the slope of the lawn, back towards the house. Then finally his mouth stretched in a quick, grim smile. "If only the memories were as easy to dig out as fragments of a musket ball. But yes, I was."

"If you should ever wish to speak of it—" I began.

But Edward shook his head. "I don't." He spoke almost sharply. "I don't even wish to *think* of it again. Napoleon's defeated. The war's over and done. I'm not going to burden you, of all people, with talk of it." He rubbed his forehead as though it ached. But then he shook his head. "I do owe you an apology, though. For the night of the masquerade. Since I came back, I—" he paused, seeming to search for words. "I can't always keep from losing my temper. Especially when there's a threat to anyone I . . . anyone I care about involved. But that's no reason I should have acted such a boor with you. I'm sorry."

For an instant, I did feel a flicker of resentment, because it felt as though he was still treating me as a child—shutting me out and refusing even to speak of whatever memories trouble him even still.

But perhaps that is not fair. Sometimes talking does not do any good. And I know when I'm upset or grieving, I want to run away to a corner by myself and hide, not speak of my feelings to anyone else.

"I'm sorry, too," I finally said.

Edward offered me his hand. "Friends again?"

I put my hand into his. "Friends."

For a moment, there was quiet between us. I'd been sketching, so I wasn't wearing gloves—and neither was Edward. I had to work to keep my pulse from racing at the feel of his palm against mine, to keep my heart from throbbing. Friends, he had said. He had taken my hand as a friend, that was all. He would not feel even a flicker of the fire that seemed to be coursing up and down my arm.

Edward's eyes were on mine. The sunlight still gilded the stubble of beard on his jaw as his fingers tightened around my hand. "Georgiana, I . . . "

Just for a moment, I felt a tiny spark of hope flicker to life. Maybe he was about to tell me that the engagement to Miss Graves was a false rumour—or had been broken off. Maybe—

Then Edward stopped. Dropped my hand to rub his forehead again. "I'm not sure how to put this. I'm not sure whether I even *should*. But I . . . I think I have to say this. I"—he raised his head to look up at me—"I do care about you, Georgiana. I—"

My pulse stopped racing and even the fire died to ash as my stomach gave a sickening drop. The tiny, irrational spark of hope I had felt only made it worse— because I knew as certainly as though I had a true gypsy fortune teller's gift what Edward was about to say next: *I do care about you, and it hasn't escaped my notice that you seem to be in love with me. And since I don't want to hurt your feelings or lead you on, I feel it only right to tell you that I'm engaged to someone else.*

And I absolutely couldn't sit there and listen to another kind, honourable, and above all, *humiliating* word.

I jumped to my feet and said, "That's so very kind

of you, Edward, thank you, but it's getting late, now—I should get back to the house."

I said it so quickly that I think actually what came out of my lips was more like, *soverykindthankyouit'sgettinglategetbacktothehouse.*

But I didn't care. Anything was better than sitting there and listening to him explain exactly how *not* in love with me he is.

Edward looked—I'm not sure how he looked. Taken aback? Puzzled?

At least he was too polite to look relieved that I'd spared him the trouble of finishing his speech. He just sat there a moment. Then he offered to carry my folding chair for me.

He scarcely spoke at all as we walked back across the lawn. And when we reached the house, he didn't come in—just said 'good day' very quietly and walked off, back towards the woods again.

Friday 27 May 1814

After yesterday, I feel as though I should have used up all my capacity for being shocked. But apparently I have not, because I am utterly shocked again now. Shocked and grieved—because this is yet another tangle that I cannot see any way of making right. Or not entirely right, at least.

This morning, M. de La Courcelle arrived just after breakfast to call on Aunt de Bourgh. I truly don't know what to think, seeing the two of them together. Aunt de Bourgh isn't so very much older than he, as Edward said. And she is handsome, in her stately, strong-featured way.

But it is still so utterly strange to see M. de La Courcelle kissing her hand . . . or murmuring soft words into her ear as he adjusts the cushions at her back. My aunt accepts all the attentions as her due, so far as I can see, and preens a little every time he looks at her. But it makes me feel . . . I don't know. Embarrassed for her, I suppose—and very awkward and uncomfortable about being in the same room with them.

I could see even Elizabeth felt the same. After just a few minutes of sitting with them in the morning room, our eyes met, and then almost at the same moment, both Elizabeth and I stood up. Elizabeth murmured something about allowing M. de La Courcelle and Aunt de Bourgh to continue their visit in private. And then together she and I went out.

Without even needing to speak of it, we agreed on leaving the house entirely, pausing only to gather up our shawls and bonnets in the hall.

Elizabeth drew a long breath of relief as we stepped out into the open air and began walking towards the path through the woods. "Oh, that's better," she said.

"How are you feeling?" I asked her. "Is the . . . illness worse this morning?"

Elizabeth shook her head. "No, it's a little better, if anything. Especially here, outside, where I can breathe fresh air." She smiled a little and rested her hand on the front of her blue muslin gown. "Maybe the infant's decided I've suffered enough."

I looked down at where her hand rested, though of course there's no sign of her expectations yet. "Do you suppose it's a boy or a girl?" I asked her.

"I don't know! It is fascinating to think of, though, isn't it?" Elizabeth said. She tilted her head back to look up at the canopy of leaves above us, letting her shawl slip down from her shoulders. "It's all possibility, now. Boy or girl. And whom he or she will most look like." She looked at me and smiled. "Maybe if it's a girl, she'll look like you. People say I resemble my Aunt Phillips, a bit."

"Just don't name her Georgiana," I said. "It's the most awful name to grow up with, because it's so suited to being stretched out for full effect when you've done something naughty. All those syllables! I can still hear my governess's voice when she was displeased with me: *Georg-i-AN-a!*"

Elizabeth laughed. "You, do anything you oughtn't? I don't believe it. Not even when you were small. I, on the other hand, used to go down to the farm at Longbourn and get into all sorts of mischief. Once I was balancing on the rail around the pig pen and fell in—head first, straight down into the mud. You should have heard my mother's shriek when she saw me, if you want to talk of hearing your name stretched out to full effect: *E-LIZ-a-beth Anne BEN-net!* I'm sure she wished she'd given me more than one second name so that she could have drawn it out still more."

I laughed, too—and then I heard it: from around a bend in the path up ahead, a rustle of leaves and low sound, half snuffle, half unsteadily drawn breath. Like someone in pain—or out of breath from running.

My heart stumbled—because my first thought was that George Wickham might have come back, and I could feel cold fear sliding all through me at the thought of meeting him like this, so far from the house.

But it wasn't Wickham. When we rounded the curve in the path, we saw Caroline Bingley, trying to scramble up from where she was sprawled on the ground.

Elizabeth drew in a quick breath of alarm and hurried forward. "Miss Bingley! What's happened? Are you hurt?"

Caroline must have heard us coming and been trying to run away, I think—but she had tripped on a root that grew up above the soil in that spot. The lace on her half-boot was broken, and the front of her dress was all-over dirt and leaf-mould. She was crying, too—great, wrenching sobs that sounded as though they were being torn from her chest. Her eyes were swollen and red.

She flinched away from Elizabeth's touch, scrabbling backwards in the carpet of fallen leaves. "Don't touch me!" her voice broke on another sob. "Don't look at me! Just go away and leave me, can't you?"

"Of course we can't leave you." Elizabeth crouched down beside Caroline and spoke softly. "Not like this. Where have you hurt yourself? Do you wish one of us to summon someone to carry you back to the house?"

"No!" Caroline's voice was almost wild, and she caught hold of Elizabeth's wrist. Even just by looking, I could see how hard Caroline's fingers were digging into Elizabeth's skin. "No, I don't want anyone, do you hear me! Not anyone!" She covered her face with her hands in a fresh burst of sobbing and then said, her voice almost a moan, "Oh, why can't you just leave me alone? Can't you understand, you're the last person I want to see me just now."

Elizabeth looked up at me and gave a small, helpless little shrug. I moved to kneel beside Caroline, as well, and put a hand on her arm. "Caroline?"

She didn't respond, not even by a twitch or a stiffening of muscles, so I shook her arm, just gently. "Caroline, what is all this? Can't you tell us what's the matter?"

"The matter? The matter?" Caroline raised her tear-stained face and looked from me to Elizabeth. Her blue eyes were glaring, and her voice was all at once almost angry. "The matter is that Jacques is engaged to Lady Catherine de Bourgh. He's actually going to marry that . . . that dried up, desiccated old woman! Just because she has an estate and a title. And I—" the anger vanished as Caroline's face crumpled into tears again. "And I love him!"

"Shh, shh." Elizabeth put an arm lightly around Caroline's shoulders. "He's not worth your crying this way for him. Especially not if he made you believe he cared for you, then got engaged to Lady Catherine behind your back."

"You don't understand!" Caroline drew a sobbing breath. "You don't understand at all. You don't know what I've done for him."

I saw a shadow of worry cross Elizabeth's face at that—and I felt the same alarm. With a little twist of fresh anger, as well. Because what I said to Edward is true: if Caroline had . . . what is the euphemism people usually use? If she had surrendered her honour, it is she who would suffer for it, not Jacques de La Courcelle.

Aloud, though, Elizabeth only said, as gently as before, "Tell us, then. Maybe we can help you."

"Help me." Caroline gave an angry shake of her head and then looked up at Elizabeth. "I was going to show you—you and Darcy both. You took Darcy away from me. And he didn't want me. Well, too bad for him, that's what I thought. I'd marry Jacques and be happy and show the both of you how little I cared! And now Jacques is going to marry an old woman for her money. And you offer to *help* me. Well I don't want your help." Caroline's face twisted and she almost screamed the words. Her hair was coming down and her shoulders were still shaking with sobs. "I don't want you, Mrs. Elizabeth Darcy! Just go away and leave me alone!"

Elizabeth watched her a moment, then slowly got to her feet. *She really is good*—because she did not look angry or offended, only pitying. "I think I'm doing more harm than good here, Georgiana," she said to me in an undertone. "Why don't you stay with her and see if you can get her to talk to you? I'll walk on a little way"—she gestured to the path ahead—"but I won't go too far, just in case you do need help."

For a second, I felt a moment of panic—some of the old feeling of being intimidated by Caroline Bingley to the point of being almost afraid of her. I had no idea what I could possibly say to her that would help. And it felt as though apart from Elizabeth, I must be the very last person in the world she'd want to have try.

But then I looked down at Caroline, huddled and sobbing on the ground, her blonde hair all tangled around her face and her skin reddened and splotched with crying. I nodded to Elizabeth. "All right. I'm not sure she'll speak to me, either. But I'll try."

I waited until Elizabeth was out of sight, then sat down beside Caroline, drawing my feet up and hugging my knees. "Do you . . . do you want to tell me what's wrong?" I asked.

Caroline did not answer. She did not even look up.

"It's something more than M. de La Courcelle's engagement to my aunt, is it not?"

Caroline was still silent, her shoulders hunched in stiff resentment.

I let out my breath. "You are not being entirely fair to Elizabeth, you know," I said. "She didn't take my brother from you. He was never yours to be taken."

I am not sure it was exactly the right thing to say—but it did get Caroline to speak to me. She raised her head again and gave me a sullen glare through her wet lashes. "I could have made him fall in love with me, if she hadn't come along."

"Do you really think so?"

Caroline just glowered. But then her shoulders slumped and her eyes fell.

"Besides," I said. "Is that really what you want? To be with a man who's been *made* to care for you? Wouldn't you rather . . . wouldn't you rather that he loved you with his whole heart, and of his own free will?"

Caroline wiped her eyes with her fingers—though her gloves were quite grubby and left smears of dirt on her cheeks. "Oh, what could you possibly know about it, Georgiana? What do you know about falling in love with someone—wanting him to care for you in return so desperately you feel as though your heart is going to burst with it every time you see him? And then having to watch him turn away from you and marry someone else."

For an instant, a vision from yesterday flashed before me: Edward leaning back in the grass beside my chair, legs stretched out before him, muscles pulling tight against the linen of his shirt. "What, indeed," I muttered. Caroline gave me a suspicious glance, and I said, before she could ask or say anything more, "Why don't you just tell me straight out exactly what it is you've done for M. de La Courcelle? You'll feel better if you confide in someone."

Actually, I did not know anything of the kind. But to my surprise, Caroline didn't argue.

She drew a slow breath and let it out again, and then

said in a low voice, her eyes fixed on the ground, "I stole
Lady Catherine's necklace."

I had been afraid, all the time we were speaking, that
Caroline was going to tell me she was going to have
Jacques de La Courcelle's child. And I truly did not
know what words of comfort I could have given her
then. But as it was, this revelation stunned me even
more.

"You did what?" I said.

"I stole Lady Catherine's necklace!" Caroline's gaze
lifted again, her chin jutting out in a challenge. "Well,
now you know. I'm a thief. Are you going to tell your
brother? He's Justice of the Peace here, isn't he? Do
you want to tell him to have me brought before the
magistrate and put on trial?"

"Of course not!" I was still trying to take in full
import of what she had told me, but I shook my head
impatiently. "I just . . . why in the world would you do
such a thing?"

"He said he needed the money." Caroline's voice was
sullen once again. She traced a trail in the dirt with the
tip of one finger. "He was going to buy Kennelwood
Hall, as I told you. Only there was another party bid-
ding on the property, and Jacques said he needed extra
capital, and quickly, or he'd lose his chance at the place.
So he asked me to take the pearls."

"He asked you to steal my aunt's pearl necklace?" I
repeated. "Just like that?"

"Yes. But it wasn't—it wasn't like you make it sound."
Caroline looked guilty and defiant, both. "Jacques was
going to give them back. He just needed them to show
the estate agent as proof that he had the means to buy
the place. Because there wasn't time for him to draw on
the property he has still tied up in France."

For a moment, I could only stare at Caroline. Did she actually believe what she said? I still do not know, even writing this now. I am very sure that she wished to believe it, at least—and it is frightening what lies people can make themselves certain of, just because they are determined to accept the lies as true.

"Have you spoken to M. de La Courcelle since he and my aunt announced their engagement?" I finally asked Caroline.

"Of course not! He's nothing but a fortune-hunting mercenary and I never want to see him or speak to him again!" Just for a moment, there was a flash of Caroline's usual self in her words and look. But then her chin trembled and fresh tears pooled in her eyes. "And yet I can't blame him, Georgiana. How can I? He's lost so much in his life—his family, his home, the position and stature that should have been his. All lost to those wicked Jacobins in France. Surely anyone can understand why he might wish to regain a little of all he once had, even if it means marrying Lady Catherine."

It was on the tip of my tongue to tell Caroline, *Don't bother with making excuses for him.* But I managed to swallow the words. If Caroline had managed to excuse both his making a thief of her *and* his engagement, I couldn't imagine what I could say that would sway her opinion against him.

She would only say I was determined to think ill of M. de La Courcelle.

It truly *is* frightening what people can persuade themselves into believing when they're in love.

I did manage to get Caroline to come with me back to the house. I took her in through the kitchen garden door and then up the servants' staircase so that there wasn't the least chance of her meeting either Aunt de Bourgh or Jacques de La Courcelle on her way to her bedroom.

I offered to sit with her, but she said that she only wanted to be left alone. So I left her there to rest if she could. And I told her that I'd ask Mrs. Reynolds to see that supper was brought up to her on a tray, so that she need not come downstairs if she did not want to face the rest of the company.

Caroline nodded dully and said that she'd already written to her sister, Mrs. Hurst, to say that she wished to leave Pemberley and join Mrs. Hurst and her husband at their home in Bath. She plans to depart as soon as the Hursts can send a carriage for her, which she thinks should be within a day or two.

It probably is for the best that she go. I'm not sure what more I or anyone else here can do for Caroline.

But here is the thought that's stuck in my mind and won't be dislodged: There seems nothing I can do for Caroline. But maybe what she's told me has given me the means to help my cousin Anne.

I'm tempted to write that *someone* may as well find love and happiness at Pemberley this spring. But that seems unfair to Anne, as well as unkind.

Edward took one of my brother's hunting rifles and stayed out of doors all day. I only saw him at dinner time. Again.

Saturday 28 May 1814

I've done it.

I still cannot entirely believe it, even now that I'm back in my own room, sitting at my writing table. It feels as though I must have either dreamt the last half an hour or stepped into someone else's skin.

But I did it—I confronted Aunt de Bourgh.

I scarcely slept at all last night. I had made up my mind even before I got into bed what I was going to have to do. I suppose I knew all along, from the moment the idea occurred to me, that I had no choice. But I still kept tossing and turning and staring around my darkened bedroom, going over and over again what I planned to say. I would mouth the words in the dark: *Aunt de Bourgh, there is something of a very serious nature that I think you must know.*

And then I would go cold all over at the thought of actually speaking them to my aunt's face.

Still, first thing this morning, I knocked on my aunt's bedroom door.

Aunt de Bourgh was sitting at the dressing table in her lace-trimmed combing jacket—though Dawson must already have finished combing her hair, because it was pinned up in its usual heavy coils. She was giving orders to Dawson about what she meant to wear that morning: "No, not the green dimity. The grey Paris muslin, I think. With the grey slippers and my cashmere shawl."

I suppose it was always futile to hope that my aunt's engagement might have softened her. She looked just as always, brows drawn in a frown above her prominent features, eyes as sharp and hard as ever.

She looked up when I came in and rapped out an impatient, "What is it, Georgiana? What do you want?"

I swallowed. It sounds silly to write it now—because of all the feats of bravery humans have achieved, facing Aunt de Bourgh scarcely registers on the scale of courage. But just for a second, I felt completely frozen at the thought of what I had come here to do. Every single one of the words I had rehearsed the night before seemed to have fled, leaving my mind entirely blank.

"Well?" my aunt said.

I swallowed again. "Aunt de Bourgh, there is something of a very serious nature that I think you must know."

"Well?" Aunt de Bourgh said again.

I took a breath. "I know who stole your pearls."

The line between my aunt's brows deepened. "Are you growing addled in your wits, Georgiana? You informed me of this already. Sir John Huntington took my pearls. And I have written both to my solicitor and to his mother—"

"No, Aunt de Bourgh." My aunt's lips thinned at the interruption, but I went on. "It wasn't Sir John Huntington who took your pearls after all. I was mistaken. It was Caroline Bingley."

Aunt de Bourgh frowned. "What? Nonsense! How do you know?"

"Because she told me." My throat still felt dry and my hands cold, but I had at least passed beyond the point where I could turn back. "I found her crying in the woods yesterday and she confessed the whole."

"She confessed? Then why has she not come to me herself?" Two angry spots of colour burned on my aunt's cheeks, and her nostrils flared. "She needn't think that she will escape the consequences of her actions. I shall see that she is prosecuted to the full extent possible by law. Perhaps if she returns the pearls directly, I may be inclined to speak to the magistrate on her behalf—"

I had to dig my fingers hard into the palms of my hands to make myself do it, but I broke into the torrent of angry words. "No, Aunt de Bourgh," I said again.

"No? What do you mean, *no*? If you think—"

"You can't prosecute Caroline Bingley," I said.

Maybe I should have found a more diplomatic way

of saying it. I doubt anyone has said, *You can't* to Aunt de Bourgh in the last thirty years or more. The angry spots in her cheeks flushed darker yet and white dents appeared on either side of her mouth as she raised her eyebrows.

"Oh, can't I? I assure you, Georgiana, that I both can and will. Who are the Bingley family, after all? Mere upstarts. I happen to know they made all their money in trade!"

"That may be, but you still cannot bring charges against Caroline." My throat cramped and sickness slid through the pit of my stomach, but I made myself go on. "Because she stole your necklace at the instigation of M. de La Courcelle."

For an instant, my aunt's bedroom was entirely still. I could hear every beat of my heart, every one of my aunt's breaths. Every soft rustle of Dawson's dress as she pressed herself quietly back into the corner—I suppose for fear my aunt would recollect her presence and order her from the room before she could hear the whole.

Then my aunt said in a low, dangerous tone, "*What* did you say?"

I moistened my lips. "I said that it was Jacques de La Courcelle who asked Caroline to steal your necklace, Aunt de Bourgh. He told her that he needed ready money to make a bid to purchase Kennelwood Hall."

I will not write down the whole of what my aunt said in response. Screamed, rather. Her furious tirade was almost the equal of the outburst when she first learned her pearls were missing. She called me every name she could think of—liar, sneak, insolent, jealous, ungrateful, headstrong girl—and said she was ashamed to call me her niece, that I was a disgrace to my parents' memory, that she was grateful her sister Anne hadn't lived to see her daughter maliciously lying to slander an innocent man—

There was a good deal more, besides. And standing there in the face of it all, at first my insides felt as though I'd swallowed broken glass, and I was sick and shaking all over with the urge to tell my aunt that Yes, of course I was mistaken or lying or simply delusional in my claims.

But then, all at once, I was not afraid at all any more. It was amazing—as though I were a clockwork figure, and someone had turned a key and shut off all fear at the source.

I was only standing a few paces away from Aunt de Bourgh, but suddenly I felt as though I were seeing her from a great distance. She seemed suddenly smaller. Small and a little ridiculous—like an overgrown child throwing a tantrum over not getting the last cream cake on the tea tray. And very pitiable, too.

I remembered what Elizabeth had said. And all at once I felt nothing but sorry for Aunt de Bourgh. Because underneath all her pride and vanity and disagreeable manners, she was at heart so desperate for someone to love her that she fell prey to the first smooth, pleasant-spoken confidence trickster of a fortune hunter who crossed her path.

Is M. de La Courcelle even French? I do not think I would be surprised to learn that he has never set foot on the Continent in his life. I keep remembering his blank look when I spoke French to him at the Herrons'.

At any rate, Aunt de Bourgh finally wound down. She looked a little disconcerted because I had not said anything, all the time she was shouting at me. She drew a breath and pressed a lace trimmed handkerchief to her mouth and said, "Well? What have you to say for yourself?"

"Only this." I did not even have to work to make my voice sound quiet and calm. "If you have such perfect confidence in Jacques de La Courcelle's honour and honesty, confront him with what I've told you yourself— let him deny my claims. See whether you are convinced by his response."

There was another silence. Slowly, the colour drained from my aunt's face, leaving her skin splotched and sallow-looking. The muscles of her throat contracted as she swallowed.

"Yes." I nodded. "I thought so." It felt brutal to take advantage of her at such a time. But I had come here for a purpose. I drew in my breath. "Your announcement of the engagement is already on its way to the *Times*. If you denounce M. de La Courcelle now, you yourself will be dishonoured by the scandal."

My aunt's tongue moved over her lips and she swallowed again. "Why do you tell me this? What do you want?"

"Your daughter Anne wishes to marry Mr. Carter," I said. "I want you to give her your blessing and consent."

My muscles had tightened in anticipation of another outburst, another angry tirade and spate of argument. But to my astonishment, my aunt simply sat, perfectly still, watching me from hooded dark eyes. Then she inclined her head. "Very well."

I must have blinked, or made some other show of surprise, because Aunt de Bourgh said, "I am her mother, Georgiana. And I am not quite a fool."

I waited, wondering whether Anne and I had been wrong about that, as well—whether my aunt did indeed feel more affection for Anne than she let show. But Aunt de Bourgh only drew herself up, straightening her shoulders beneath the lacy folds of the combing jacket. Her colour was still bad, but she said, with something of a return to her usual manner, "You may go, now, Georgiana. And I trust we need not speak of these matters again."

She was strangely admirable, in that moment—oddly, more impressive I think than I had ever found her before.

Monday 30 May 1814

Caroline left this morning, her brother-in-law's carriage having arrived to fetch her. And Aunt de Bourgh wore her pearl necklace at dinner tonight. I think the entire company of us stared when she came downstairs, but she only said, before anyone could ask questions, that she had discovered that she'd simply misplaced her pearls, after all. They had slipped down inside an inner pocket in her jewel case, but she had found them, now, and all was well.

M. de La Courcelle came to dinner again. Dressed in an embroidered velvet coat and white satin waistcoat that I am very sure he knew set off his dark good looks. He did not look at all guilty or conscious. But he *was* more attentive to my aunt than ever: making sure she had a sample of every dish on the table, insisting that he change places with her on the sofa in the drawing room afterwards, because, he said, he was sure that she was sitting in a draft.

Aunt de Bourgh accepted his attentions just as regally and graciously as before—except that she looked at him from time to time and touched the pearls around her throat.

I've been pitying my aunt—but maybe it should have

been Jacques de La Courcelle for whom I felt sorry, because I think that in marrying Aunt de Bourgh he may get more than he bargained for.

Edward spent most of yesterday and today out of doors again, first in shooting and then he and my brother rode out to look over the tenant farms and timberlands. He was perfectly pleasant and good tempered at dinner—but he did not look at me at all, much less speak to me.

Even Elizabeth noticed it, and asked whether Edward and I had quarrelled. I said—truthfully—that we had not.

Part of me wished I could tell Elizabeth. But I couldn't bring myself to.

I really *can't* blame Edward for not wishing to speak of past battles to me. Though I suppose the cases are not exactly parallel.

But there has been one utterly happy result: This morning I went to my cousin Anne's room, even before the hour when we usually meet for dancing practice.

Anne's face was pale, and her eyelids looked puffy and reddened, as though she had been crying. But she smiled a little when I asked her how she was. "As well as can be expected, considering that I'm about to gain a step-father who is only five or six years older than I am myself."

"Do you mind about your mother and M. de La Courcelle?" I asked. I had not fully realised it before—but of course the engagement would affect Anne more than anyone else.

She shook her head, though. "I don't think I do. Not really." The faint ghost of a smile touched her mouth again. Not a bitter smile, exactly, only sad. "At the very least, it will give my mother someone else in the house to bully and manage. I just wish—" she stopped and looked away.

"I've come to tell you something," I said. And then I recounted the whole: Caroline's confession, my interview with Aunt de Bourgh the day before.

Anne's swollen eyes widened as I spoke. "You said *what?*" she said when I had finally done. And then: "And my mother actually . . . she actually *agreed?*"

"She did," I said.

"I—" Anne shook her head. "I don't know what to say." She was sitting quite still. And yet her face looked . . . *free.* That's the only word I can find to describe it. She looked like someone stepping out-of-doors on the first day of spring, or passing out through a prison gate and into the sun. She shook her head again. "It's almost too much to take in."

"You can tell Mr. Carter—" I began.

I could almost hear a thud as Anne seemed to come back to earth. She stared at me, her eyes still wide. "But I can't—I mean, I couldn't do that! How would it sound? And what on earth could I say? *My mother has agreed to our marriage if you should like to propose to me?* How can I tell him anything? It would sound so dreadfully bold."

I had been trying my hardest to squash down any jealousy I might feel for Anne. I did—I do—want her to be happy, and it was not fair to envy her for actually having that happiness within her reach.

But all at once, looking at her, I felt every bit of misery and temper and heartache I had ever felt over Edward and George Wickham and Mr. Edgeware and my brother and Elizabeth and *everything* come churning up from inside me in a hot, furious wave.

"Oh for goodness' sake, Anne, *will* you stop being

such an incurable ninny!" My chest was so tight I felt as though it would split open. "You're lucky enough to fall in love with someone who actually loves you in return—and you're willing to lose all chance of happiness with him because you're afraid of sounding *forward*? Very well! Go back to Rosings and live under your mother's thumb for the rest of your life, and you can comfort yourself with the knowledge that you were always the essence of decorum and propriety!"

Anne's jaw had dropped open. She closed her mouth, swallowed, then opened it again. "I'll . . . I'll speak to John," she finally said.

"Good."

The wildfire burn of anger was fading from my veins. I let out my breath and almost despite myself felt a small, reluctant smile forming at the corners of my lips at the realisation of how I must have looked. "I'm sorry, Anne," I said. "I didn't mean to barge into your room—before breakfast, even—and shout at you like a fish-wife."

Anne smiled—then started to laugh. "That's all right. I suppose I *was* being stupid. And very irritating, be-sides. I—" and then she stopped, looking at me closely.

"What is it?" I asked.

"I was just wondering why you bothered," Anne said. She was still watching me. "Why you bothered to speak to my mother for me, and take me out on carriage rides and teach me to dance and make me go to the ball and . . . and all the rest. We have never been friends. And you cannot say it was because you liked me or enjoyed my company."

I tried to think of an answer. I was not sure whether Anne would be angry or no, but finally I said, "Maybe not at first. But I am glad now that I did—because I do like you now. And as for why I bothered in the first place I suppose it was because—" I stopped, then told her what I'd realised before. "Because I think we are alike, in many ways."

As it turned out, Anne didn't look angry—only thoughtful. Her blue eyes seemed to search me a long moment. And then she said, "Maybe we are. But what about you, Georgiana? You've"—she smiled a little again—"persuaded me into finding a chance of happiness. But what about you? Don't you want anything for yourself?"

I was surprised. Truly, nearly as surprised as when Aunt de Bourgh announced her engagement. I think perhaps that is the most miraculous change of all: Anne caring enough to be concerned for someone besides herself.

She really *is* different from the sickly invalid who never spoke or seemed to think of anything or anyone besides her own health. Or maybe she always was, and it is just that she never showed anyone this other side of her before.

For a moment, I wanted to confide in her—nearly as much as I wished I could tell Elizabeth. And that is yet another unexpected turn, because I should never have guessed that Anne would turn into someone I might truly want for a friend.

But I did not tell her, all the same.

Which I hope was more because I did not wish to spoil her happiness than because I envied her.

I shook my head and made myself smile and said, "What do I want? What I can't have—I suppose like most of us in this world."

Anne just looked at me another moment. And then

she said, "You know, Georgiana, you're not at all what I thought you were. I remember when you were small—I suppose I was fourteen or fifteen and you four or five— you were so shy I almost never heard you speak or saw you when you weren't hiding behind someone's skirts. Even from when we first arrived at Pemberley a few weeks ago—you've changed. Or at least, you're very different from what I first thought."

"Well, so are you," I told her. And then—on impulse— I hugged her. "I *am* happy for you, Anne. Truly."

Anne stiffened as though I had startled her. But then she hugged me in return and said, "Now, is there time for one last dancing practice before breakfast? I want to make sure I don't disgrace myself—or your teaching— at the ball tomorrow night." She smiled. "It was much easier at the masquerade—then I was wearing a mask and had the comfort of knowing that if I fell out of step, no one would know who I was."

I just stared at her. But she is right—the ball here at Pemberley is to be held tomorrow night. I can scarcely believe it, but with everything else that has happened these last days, I had almost forgotten it was to be held at all.

Anne and I did go down to the music room to prac- tice. Mr. Folliet joined us as usual. He was called away partway through our session by an urgent message that Mrs. Reynolds came to tell him had just arrived for him. He looked very serious as he left the room—as though he expected whatever the message was to contain bad news.

But he made both Anne and me promise to save him a dance.

Tuesday 31 May 1814

I suppose actually I should strike out that 31 May and write in 1 June instead, for it's three o'clock in the morning. But I hate the look of ink blots and scratched-out words.

My feet ache from so many hours of dancing—and I should be tired enough to sleep for a week. But somehow every time I try to lie down, my mind starts flashing through the events of the ball again—like one of those pictures-in-motion flip books I used to have when I was small.

So I'm sitting up in bed to write this, with a candle lighted by my bedside.

I'm sure Aunt de Bough would scold me over the risk of fire, if I should knock the candle over onto the blankets or sheets or bed hangings. But I'm too tired to move. So if this diary should be found burned to a cinder along with me and the bed, whoever finds it will know it was my own fault.

Well, they will if this final entry is still legible, I mean.

I wore the new ballgown tonight—the peach silk with its gauze overdress and embroidered rosebuds. The sleeves are pointed lace, trimmed with tiny seed pearls, and I had a ribbon trimmed with the same pearls woven through my hair. Anne came to my room when it was time to go downstairs. She had on a ball gown that I'm certain Aunt de Bourgh must have had made for her— the only ball gown she had in her trunk, I suppose: a pea green satin with a yellow lace overdress, trimmed with gold braid and spangles. She had a bandeau of the same pea green satin around her hair, trimmed with a spray of feathers.

But she looked so happy that even the gown couldn't spoil her looks; I did not even need to ask to know she must already have spoken to Mr. Carter.

We went downstairs to the drawing room together. My brother and Elizabeth were already there, Elizabeth looking lovely in a gown of sea-blue silk, with a silver net overskirt, and silver embroidery around the neck and the hem. Her family arrived this afternoon–only her father and her sisters Mary and Kitty, since her mother was feeling unwell and unable to make the journey.

And Edward was there, as well. Dressed in his military uniform, of course: red coat and cream-coloured breeches, with the medal he won at Vimeiro pinned to his chest.

At least the carriages began to arrive almost as soon as Anne and I came down, and we were so busy with greeting the guests who were presented in turn that I was spared having to speak to him.

I had been dreading that part of the evening—having to greet everyone and shake hands and try to think of polite conversation to make with so many people that I do not know very well at all. Between my brother's acquaintances and those of Aunt de Bourgh, there were more than a hundred families invited. Some of them I could not even remember having met with before.

But as it turned out, it was not nearly so bad as I had feared.

Maybe Anne was right, and I really have changed.

Mr. and Mrs. Herron arrived first, and that helped— they were both of them so unaffected and truly kind. Maria has gone back home to her family, and they miss her terribly. Though Mrs. Herron said she would be back for a visit in the summer, because it appears she didn't manage to get engaged after all.

Which made me smile—but I do sincerely wish her well.

After the guests had all arrived, we went into the ballroom—which looked magical, all decked with garlands of flowers and with potted palms arranged in the corners and candles glowing in the chandeliers and sconces on the walls.

I opened the ball dancing with my brother—and of course a set of dancers formed from the neighbourhood families we know best, and Mr. Carter and Anne, who lined up below Fitzwilliam and me as we stood at the top of the room. And I was concentrating so hard on not tripping or forgetting a step—or looking at all the people watching—that it was all over almost before I realised.

After that I was partnered by Mr. Folliet—who came to remind me that I had promised him a dance. And then—

But I can scarcely remember them all, I danced so many sets. That part of the evening was lovely. It was. Of course, I knew quite well that a solid half of my partners would not have danced with me at all, save for the size of my fortune. But somehow being well aware of the fact meant that it did not trouble me nearly as much as it might once have done.

And some of the quieter, more serious ones looked at me with real admiration in their eyes. At least, I think it must have been real, because they didn't try to be charming or pay me compliments out loud or beg a place beside me at supper. Which was nice, to realise that the world is not entirely composed of fortune hunters.

And yet—

I'd told myself I was not going to stare at Edward all

evening like some lovesick schoolgirl. He had not even spoken to me at any time during the day to ask me to save him a dance.

But you know how it is when you have told yourself you absolutely must not take any notice of someone—and that only makes you want to look in their direction even more?

I felt as though every nerve in my body were strung tight with awareness of exactly where he was. His red coat of course made him easy to spot among the crowd of guests; there weren't many other army officers there. But I did not even need that. My skin prickled every time he came within twenty paces of where I stood, and my neck muscles ached with the wish to turn in his direction.

At last, I finally did turn.

Elizabeth was feeling a little tired, and I had sat down beside her on one of the couches around the dancing floor to keep her company while she rested. I could feel Edward's presence behind me, and when I looked to the left, I could just see him out of the corner of my eye as he stood talking to some of the other guests.

I couldn't help it—one of the older ladies stopped to say something to Elizabeth, and while they were speaking I turned in Edward's direction. And found him staring at me, with the strangest look on his face and an expression I could not read at all in his dark eyes.

He said something—an apology, maybe—to the stout matron in pearl-grey with whom he had been speaking. And then he started towards me, his eyes still holding mine.

I felt my heart give a strange little lurch and my pulse quicken. But before Edward reached Elizabeth's and my sofa, Mr. Carter had come up on my other side. "Miss Darcy, may I—m-m-may I speak to you?"

He seemed so much agitated that I was frightened something had happened or gone wrong between him and Anne. I stood up and went with him into a quieter alcove of the ballroom, at the far end of the room away from the musicians hired for the evening.

"Mr. Carter, what is it? Is something amiss?"

Nothing was, of course. He *had* spoken to Anne—or rather Anne had spoken to him, earlier in the day. And he had simply wanted to come and thank me in person for all I had done.

I told him it was nothing and that I was happy to have been of help. And offered him every felicitation on his engagement to Anne. For they are engaged—he gave me the news himself—and are to be married as soon as he can find a new vicarage.

I *am* very happy for them.

But when I came out from the alcove, Edward was nowhere to be seen.

It was not until it was time to go in to supper that I saw him again. This time, I actually had not been at all aware of where he was. I was being pushed on the tide of guests moving from the ballroom to the supper room, and I almost walked straight into him. I drew back so sharply to keep from colliding with him that I nearly lost my balance. He had to steady me with a hand on my elbow.

The other attendants to the ball were streaming past us on either side; Edward moved us back towards the wall, out of the worst of the traffic—and he still had to raise his voice to be heard over the noise.

"Georgiana, I—" he began.

But then a stout, elderly gentleman in a green velvet

jacket and old-fashioned wig actually *did* carom straight into Edward, separating us. I did recognise the older gentleman—though I don't know him well. His name is Colonel George Wylton. He lives on an estate near Klimpton, and he earned his army title commanding a regiment in the American colonies during the war for independence.

"Eh, what?" Colonel Wylton squinted at Edward from port-bleared eyes. "Ah, Fitzwilliam! But what luck—I was just looking for you. I never got to finish telling you about what happened during the battle at Norfolk. Got some stories that would curl your hair, I can tell you. Townspeople wouldn't surrender their provisions to us—had to eat rats and whatever else we could catch for days. I—"

I lost the rest of what he said as he carried Edward off with him into the supper room. Edward did look back at me—once—but by then there were ten or more people in between us, and no chance of exchanging another word.

Mr. Folliet sat beside me at supper; he had held a chair for me, and asked whether I would sit with him the moment I came into the room. He was very quiet, though, his handsome face thoughtful and grave and not like his usual manner at all.

When we had finished our plates of mayonnaise of chicken and pineapple cream, he turned to me and said, "Miss Darcy, I realise this may not be the most opportune time, but may I . . . may I speak to you? Privately, I mean? There's something of a . . . there is something I need to ask you."

I did feel some apprehension, because for a moment I wondered whether he was going to propose—and that would spoil our friendship. But I said, "Of course.

Come outside into the garden. It will be quiet there."

Strictly speaking, it might not have been entirely proper for me to go outside alone with Mr. Folliet. But if I were going to be forced to refuse him, I could not stand for it to be under the eyes of some hundred or more guests at the ball.

And the garden *was* quiet. Quiet and cool after the heat and noise inside. For a moment, I just stood quite still, feeling the soft night breeze on my skin, breathing in the scent of the flowers and freshly clipped grass. Then I turned to Mr. Folliet, bracing myself a little for fear of whatever he was about to say. But his first words were, "The message that arrived for me yesterday. It was from my grandfather. The Earl of Blaisdon."

"Oh." I felt a quick rush of relief. Because if it were to be a proposal, this was surely the oddest beginning for one I had ever heard.

"Or rather, I should say that it was from my grandfather's estate agent. My grandfather can't write anymore, his hands are so crippled by his rheumatism. He's been in poor health for years. But he is failing seriously, now. The message I received yesterday said that his physician doubts he can last more than a month. Perhaps not even so long."

"I am so sorry," I said.

I could see lines of worry and grief about the corners of Mr. Folliet's mouth. But he forced a smile. "Thank you. I'm fond of the old boy. He practically raised me, after my parents died. He's been good to me always. Even when I was fifteen with spots and enough vanity of my own opinions and intelligence to make two of the Emperor Napoleon."

Mr. Folliet fell silent a moment, staring at the shadows cast by a lilac bush. Then he suddenly said, "Do you remember, the night of the masquerade ball, I asked whether I might I ask you a question? But then I never got the chance to finish. Do you think I might ask it now?"

I nodded. "Of course."

Mr. Folliet didn't speak at once, though. He rubbed a hand across the back of his neck and then finally said, half under his breath, "I actually have no idea how to put this. But all right." He swung round to face me. "My question is this: are you in love with me?"

I was so utterly taken aback—and then sick with apprehension, because it seemed he was going to press his suit after all—that I couldn't find a word to say. I just stood there, feeling as though the words to every polite denial I tried to frame . . . *I'm deeply sensible of the honour . . . I do like you very much* . . . were like water droplets, sliding through my grasp.

But Mr. Folliet, studying my face, let out a long breath of relief and said, "Ah, thank God. You're not."

If I had been surprised before, it was nothing to what I felt now. Mr. Folliet laughed at my expression. "I'm sorry. I didn't think you were. But I had to be sure. I—" He stopped and then turned and offered me his arm. "But shall we walk a little. I will explain, I swear it. And ask your help, if you are of a mind to give it. It's just I feel as though this might be easier to speak of while I'm in motion."

I was still thoroughly puzzled. But I did take his arm, and we started to walk along one of the garden paths. "It's like this," Mr. Folliet finally said. "My grandfather's dearest wish is—and has been for some time—to see me married. It's been a continued grief to him that I haven't yet found a wife. The trouble is"—Mr. Folliet stopped, and rubbed the back of his neck again. "The trouble is that I'm not . . . not of the marrying inclination. If you see what I mean."

It took me a moment to understand, but then I did. "I—oh." I frowned. "And your . . . your grandfather the earl doesn't know?" I asked.

Mr. Folliet was watching me, with something between amusement and surprised relief in his eyes. "That's all? Just 'oh'? No screams of horror? Not even a gasp of alarm?"

"Not for the present, at any rate. I promise I'll give you fair warning if I do feel any screams coming on."

Mr. Folliet laughed again, some of the lines of tension on his face loosening their grip. "Fair enough." He sobered almost at once, though, and said, "As for my grandfather, no, he doesn't know. I've never told him. I—" he stopped. "He's all the family I have . . . and I'm all he has. I didn't want to be a disappointment to him. Even when he's asked me when I'm going to bring my bride home to meet him, I've always been too much of a coward to tell him the truth."

Mr. Folliet's words from the first conversation we'd ever had came back to me. I said, "I think just as you said, it's not always easy to be honest with family. Especially the ones we love best."

Mr. Folliet shook his head. "I always meant to, one day. I would have. At least I hope I would have. But then his health began to fail, and—and now I can't tell him the truth. The shock might be enough to kill him outright. And he'd never have time to grow accustomed to the news—to accept it, if he could. Telling him now would only mean that he'd die angry and bitterly disappointed in the boy he'd raised almost as a son."

I touched Mr. Folliet's hand. "I do understand. Truly. But you spoke of asking my help. What is it I can do for you?"

Mr. Folliet looked away, back towards the lighted rectangles that were the house windows. "Now my grandfather is . . . dying"—he flinched a little over saying the word—"and wandering in his wits. His estate manager writes that he is greatly troubled by my not having yet found a wife. He grieves to think of me, alone in the world and without a family of my own, once he's gone. I'm planning to travel to him at once—I'll have to leave Pemberley first thing tomorrow morning. And the favour I have to ask of you is this: would you permit me to tell my grandfather that you and I are engaged? The falsehood would be for his ears only," he hastened to add. "His health doesn't permit him to leave his bedroom anymore, so he would be quite unable to speak of it to anyone else. And it's not a question of securing my inheritance or anything of that—the estate is entailed on me, regardless of my grandfather's will. But it would"— his lips tightened—"it would bring him great happiness, and enable him to die in peace, if he could spend his last days believing me engaged to Miss Georgiana Darcy of Pemberley."

"Of course," I said. I did not even need to think about my answer. "Of course you may tell him that, if you wish. You have my free and full consent."

I heard Mr. Folliet's breath go out in a rush, and then he took my hand. "Thank you," he said. He raised my hand to his lips. And then he lifted his head and looked down at me. "Is it Colonel Fitzwilliam? The man you're actually in love with?"

I felt my own breath go out as though a giant hand had struck me in the ribs. I was so utterly caught off guard that I could not even summon words to deny it. Almost before I realised the words had left my mouth, I heard myself say, "How did you know?"

One side of Mr. Folliet's mouth lifted in a wry smile. "I know a thing or two about watching someone you love but can never have. Or at least, think you can't."

"I . . . I suppose you would," I said. I turned my head to look down at the pebbled edging on one of the flower beds. "But in this case, I don't just *think*, I know. Edward doesn't . . . he doesn't feel that way about me—not the way I feel for him."

"How do you know?"

"He told me. Or as good as."

Somewhere in one of the lilac bushes, a night bird had set up a trilling song. All around us, the breeze was full of the soft whispers of leaves, the music drifting out to us from the house. "Well, then," Mr. Folliet said at last, "he's an utter fool." He squeezed my hand. "And you can tell him I said so."

That made me smile. "Thank you," I said. "That's—"

And then I broke off, my whole body freezing and my heart skittering to a stop at the voice that spoke behind us. "Georgiana!"

It was Edward. Of course. Score another for Fate's unpleasant sense of humour.

Except that in this case, it was not only Fate. Edward must have come outside after us because he was following me. Again.

And how much of what Mr. Folliet and I had been saying had Edward overheard? My heart had started again and was pounding in my chest, and I was grateful for the darkness that hid the burning blush I knew was spreading over my face.

For all I knew, Edward could have been standing there behind us long enough to hear the whole of that last exchange.

My voice was quite steady, though, as I turned to Mr. Folliet. "Would you excuse us for a moment, please?"

"Of course. Good night, Miss Darcy. And"—Mr. Folliet's eyes met mine—"Thank you. With all my heart."

He divided a bow between me and Edward and was gone almost at once, walking back towards the house.

Edward watched him, frowning. "He beats a hasty retreat."

"You can hardly blame him for that," I said. "The last time you found him with me, you punched him in the mouth." I took a breath, trying to steady my voice. Even though renewed anger had kindled inside me that Edward should have taken it on himself to follow me again. "And what do you mean by this, Edward? I thought we'd established that I do not require to be guarded like a child of six."

Edward ignored that. There was just light enough for me to see the muscle ticking in his cheek. "Are you and Folliet engaged?" he asked.

"And why is that any concern of yours?"

"Because your father left me as your guardian. And unless you're engaged to a man, it is not decent for you to be walking alone in a garden with him at night."

If Edward had said anything—practically *anything*—else, I mightn't have been so furious. But the words, combined with the knowledge that he might well have stood listening to me speaking of what I felt for him, seemed to strike my already smouldering temper like a bolt of lightning, igniting it into a blaze.

"Decent? *You're* going to stand there and lecture me about decency and propriety and respectable behaviour when you've spent the last year on army campaign? Slogging through mud and snow and sleeping on the ground and fighting battles and killing—"

I broke off—and wished I could have bitten my tongue out, because I had taken a step forward and seen Edward's face more clearly in the rays of moonlight slanting down.

I had been focusing so much all night long on not letting myself look at him . . . not following him with my eyes . . . or throwing myself in his path . . . or giving him another opportunity to give me a polite speech about how much he cares about me . . . that it hadn't occurred to me to think about what this evening must have been like for him.

He'd told me how hard he finds it to be in large crowds of company, now. How the noise and the heat and the candle smoke contrive to bring back the roar of battle.

Now his face looked so drained of colour it was like bleached bone, and his expression was the grim, tight-jawed stare of a man suffering almost unendurable pain.

"Edward, I'm sorry," I said. I took another step forward and put my hand on his arm. "I should not have said that."

"Why not?" Edward's look didn't alter, and the muscles of his arm felt like those of a stone statue under my hand. "It's true. I don't fit in with this world any more. I'm not a part of balls or dancing or talking a great deal without actually saying anything." The muscles of his jaw were still jumping, and he almost spat the words out. "I'm much better at fighting and shooting and killing than I am at being in polite society now."

"Edward, I—" I stopped. What could I possibly say? I had to try, though—that look on his face was my doing, my fault. "I don't feel myself much a part of balls and supper parties and all the rest, either. But that doesn't mean you don't belong here. You could never change so much that there wouldn't be a place for you here at Pemberley."

Edward didn't speak. My hand was still on his arm and we were standing so close together that I could see the pulse beating in his throat, but I couldn't read his expression at all.

"And I . . . I apologise for accusing you of following me," I finally said. I forced myself to speak slowly, calmly, forced the anger and resentment back down. "I know you only wish to protect me. As my brother does. I know I should be grateful to you for being willing to track down George Wickham. I am very sure that there are more pleasant ways you could have spent that week of your—"

"Devil take it!" Edward almost shouted the words. I would have taken a step backward, but he'd seized my shoulders and his hard grip held me in place. "I don't want your damned gratitude! I didn't do it so you'd be grateful!"

His fingers dug painfully into my skin, and the remote, austere mask had cracked. I had never seen Edward look so utterly furious before.

"Then why did you, Edward?" I'd meant to make the words calm, still, and steady, but they came out as barely a whisper.

Edward's eyes were locked on mine, and I saw something flicker in their depths. "I—" I saw the muscles of his throat contract as he swallowed. Then he let out a ragged breath. "You'd better go." I could see a glitter of perspiration on his brow. I felt his hands loosen their hard grip on my arms—slowly, as though he were forcing his fingers to relax one by one.

"Edward, I—" I began.

But he cut me off, his voice flat, now, but so savage it

made me take a stumbling step back. "Go, Georgiana. Go back to your ball."

I did look back over my shoulder at him just once as I walked back to the house. Edward hadn't moved. He was standing absolutely motionless, with his back straight and his shoulders rigid, looking out into the night.

He did not want me with him—he made that clear. So why have I felt ever since—and more strongly, still, writing this now—that I should have stayed? I can't stop seeing him the way he looked standing there at the last—fierce and proud and so utterly *alone* that it's making my throat ache and my heart contract just to remember it. I—

It's no use. I'm not going to be able to sleep in any case.

I'm going to set this book down and go to Edward's room. If those words look illegible, it's because my hand is gripping the pen so hard it is likely to snap in my fingers. I have no idea what I'll find when I get there. Maybe Edward will only send me away again. But I know I will not be able to live with myself if I do not at least try.

Not when I am the one who brought that look to his face, that savage note to his voice, by losing my temper and saying to him what I did.

If Edward does refuse to see me, I suppose my next diary entry will be dated half an hour from now.

Wednesday 1 June 1814

It's just a few short hours since I set this book down. It's dawn, now—or nearly so. The sky is turning from midnight blue to pearly grey, and the birds are singing.

I haven't slept yet. But I couldn't possibly even try. My slippers are stained with grass and dirt and the hem of my dressing gown is wet with the morning dew and I feel—

But I'm going to set this down properly. Maybe that will help me decide whether I have been awake or only dreamed this all.

I did go to Edward's room. My pulse was racing and I had to force myself to take every step down the long hall to the stairs. Edward's room—the new room Mrs. Reynolds found him—is one floor up from mine and over in the east wing of the house, and at each step I felt the fingers grasping my candle holder turning colder and colder with nerves.

But I would not let myself turn back. Regardless of what Edward felt for me, I knew as surely as I have ever known anything that he needed *someone* to be with him last night. And I knew equally well that he would never ask himself.

But he had sat every night with me, after my mother died. I surely owed it to him to do the same for him. Even if he was engaged to another girl—even if he never saw me as anything but his ward and friend.

My heart felt as though it were trying to hammer a way out of my chest when I finally reached Edward's door. I tapped on the door panel—just softly, but there was a response from inside at once. A sound of movement, and then Edward's voice saying, "Hello? Who's there?"

His voice sounded raspy, and I realised that he might well have been asleep. It was past three o'clock in the morning, after all. He had probably been peacefully asleep in his bed, and I had come along and awakened him.

I might have turned around and gone straight back to my own room then and there. But before I could move, the door had swung open and Edward was standing there.

"Georgiana!" His eyes were bleared, and he shook his head as though trying to clear it. "What is it? Is Elizabeth ill—or your brother—"

I shook my head before he could imagine any worse. "No, nothing like that. I just—" I stopped.

Edward must have lain down in his clothes. He wore trousers and shirt, still, but the trousers were rumpled and the shirt opened nearly to the waist. The hard planes of his muscles gleamed in the light of my candle, and I could see the knotted red line of another scar running down his ribcage.

I was feeling more than foolish by that time—and I realised as well that in deciding to go to Edward, I had given no thought whatever to what I was going to say when I actually saw him.

"I've woken you," I finally said. "I'm sorry."

Edward pushed a hand through his dishevelled hair. "Don't be." His lips curved in a quick flicker of his usual smile—though there was a grim edge to it tonight. "My dreams aren't the best of company these days."

"Is that why—" my gesture encompassed his room and the empty, darkened hall of the east wing. As Mrs. Reynolds said, none of the other rooms nearby are in use—they never are, unless we've a large party of guests to stay.

I thought first Edward was not going to answer, but then his lips flattened into a line and his fingers tightened on the door frame. "I thought it better manners not to inflict my nightmares on the other residents here. You'd soon get tired of being woken up by my shouts."

He shook his head. "But you haven't told me what you're doing here. You didn't come up here in the middle of the night to ask about my dreams."

"Actually"—I swallowed—"I did." Edward's eyebrows shot up, and I hurried on, "I thought you might . . . tonight you looked . . . " I stopped and drew in my breath, looking up into Edward's face. "I thought you looked as though you needed a friend to be with tonight. And I couldn't sleep. So here I am."

Something flickered—just for an instant—across Edward's lean face. But then he shook his head. "You wouldn't understand—" he began.

Part of me wanted to shake him and demand that he stop treating me like a child. But instead I drew another slow breath and said, softly, "You don't know that I wouldn't understand. You could at least try talking to me. I do at least know what it's like to keep all your feelings bottled up inside."

Edward's head lifted at that. Just for a moment, his eyes looked . . . longing. Vulnerable, even. But then he shook his head. "I don't think this is such a good—"

I wouldn't let him finish. I reached up to touch his cheek. "I'm not going to sit by and watch you tear yourself into pieces if I might be able to help." I stopped. "Please, Edward?" Despite myself, I heard my voice shake and felt my eyes start to sting. "I'm so truly sorry for saying . . . for saying what I said to you tonight. I couldn't bear it if it ruined our friendship. Save for my brother, you've been—you *are*—the most important person in my life."

Edward's whole body stiffened at my touch; I saw his jaw clench and his fingers curl. I almost held my breath and I counted four, then five beats of my own heart before finally his head jerked in a movement that was half nod, half shrug. "All right. But two conditions—don't ask questions. I sometimes . . . I just don't want to talk about some of it, that's all."

The warmth of relief was making my muscles feel almost limp, but I nodded. "It's all right. I'm like that, too. You don't have to talk to me at all, if you don't want to. Just let me keep you company for a while. And the second condition?"

Something flickered again across Edward's features before he rubbed a hand across his face and let out an explosive breath. "Can we go outside? I feel . . . I sometimes feel as though I can't breathe inside four walls these days."

I was only wearing my slippers and rose silk dressing gown over my nightdress. But Edward didn't seem to notice. And I didn't want to risk him changing his mind by doing anything to delay.

We went downstairs together, and when we'd stepped outside onto the lawn, I saw at least some of the tension ebb from Edward's muscles. He drew air into his lungs then turned to me. "Are you . . . do you think we could walk for a while?"

"Of course."

Edward raised one eyebrow, and there was more of his usual self in the lift at the corners of his mouth. "'Of course' to a country ramble at nearly four in the morning? Just like that?"

I smiled as well. "At least you can't lecture me about propriety this time—not without lecturing yourself."

We did not talk at all as we made our way across the lawn to the lake, and from there onto the path through the woods. The velvet dark shadows of the trees nearly blocked out the moonlight. It was so dark that I could only just dimly make out the path ahead, and Edward was just a shadowed, solid warmth beside me; I could not see his face at all.

We had been walking without touching, but before long I had stumbled over roots and fallen sticks so many times that Edward offered me his arm and I took it, leaning against him for balance when I tripped for what must have been the fourth or fifth time.

"How is it you can see well enough to keep from falling?" I asked.

"Practice." I could imagine Edward's grimace, even if I could not see his face. "Too many forced retreats under cover of darkness."

I wanted to ask him more—to know where the retreats had been, and what had happened to him and his men. But I had promised not to, so we went along in silence for a time.

And then, quite suddenly, Edward said—almost as though the words were torn out of him—"After a battle, there's a roll call. To see who's missing. And then all the women whose husbands have been missed come up to the front of the lines to ask the surviving men if they know anything. There was one woman—Mrs. Harris— I'd been next to her husband in the battle at Toulouse. I'd seen him fall. She asked me to take her to the place. In case he was only wounded, and might yet be saved. So I brought her to the spot on the battlefield. Through all the . . . all the piles of the dead and the groaning wounded men. I—" Edward stopped, and I heard him clear his throat. "Harris was alive. Just. Too far gone to speak, though. And no chance of him surviving. All we could do was . . . was sit there, and watch him die."

Edward's voice was tight with control, but still there was a note in it that made me press his arm more tightly and say, "At least she had you with her—Mrs. Harris,

I mean. At least she had the comfort of not having to bear it on her own."

"Comfort," Edward repeated. He gave a harsh laugh, a bitter sound without even a trace of humour. "She didn't think so. She kept screaming at me, 'It should have been you! You were right beside him! Why couldn't you have been the one to die?' And all I could think"—Edward stopped, and I heard him swallow in the dark—"All I could think, standing there on the field of battle was: *My God, she's right*. Harris had a wife and family—they had two young children together. And there's me, unmarried—not even my father's only son. Of the two of us, I *should* have been the one to die."

I couldn't find a word to say. What was there I possibly *could* say that would be any help? Any words I tried out silently in my head sounded empty and worse than pointless. And yet, I couldn't bear the pain in Edward's voice.

Before I could lose my courage, I turned and put my arms around him, holding him tightly. He stiffened again; his muscles rigid and unyielding. Then he let out a ragged breath. "Georgiana, I can't . . . you need to run away again."

I could feel his heart beating hard against my cheek. "Why?"

"Because if you don't"—Edward's voice was husky—"because if you don't, I'm not going to be able to stop myself from doing this."

His hands came up, sliding along my jaw to tangle in my hair, tilting my face up to his. He brought his mouth down on mine and kissed me. His arms were solid and strong around me, his lean body hard against mine—and yet his lips were so soft, gentle and warm. In the darkness, without sight, everything was pure sensation.

I felt as though my bones were melting, as though every nerve in my body had come alive at his touch.

It took every scrap of will I had to brace my hands against Edward's chest and push him away. "We can't!" I heard how unsteady the words sounded.

Edward's voice was uneven as well, and he was breathing as though he'd been running. "I'm sorry. God, I—" and then he took hold of my hand, pulling me close to him again. I could just make out the outlines of his head and shoulders above mine. "*Are* you engaged to Folliet?"

"No." I shook my head, even though he couldn't see it in the dark.

"In love with him, then?" Edward's voice still sounded rough.

"No, of course not. Nor he with me. That was what he wanted to speak to me about tonight at the ball. To make sure I was not in love with him."

"To make sure you were not—" Edward began.

But I stopped him before he could finish. I felt as though the words were hot coals, burning my mouth; I couldn't speak them fast enough. "That's not why we can't . . . I can't . . . I'm not engaged to Mr. Folliet or anyone else. But you are."

I felt rather than saw Edward's raised brows. There was a space of silence, and then he said, sounding almost back to normal, "I'm engaged to Mr. Folliet? Do you know, I should have thought that would be the kind of thing I'd be able to remember."

My chest was too tight for me to smile, though. "I don't mean that. I meant that you're *engaged*. To Miss Mary Graves."

"I'm—good Lord, where did you hear that?" In the dark, I had only his voice to go by, but he didn't sound guilty or conscious. Only utterly surprised.

"Elizabeth's sister Kitty wrote and told her so. Isn't it"—I had to swallow before I could trust my own voice—"Isn't it true?"

"True? I should say not. Listen to me, Georgiana. No, better yet"—he took my arm and turned us both back the way we'd come—"keep walking and listen to me. I'm not and never have been engaged to Mary Graves. She's the sister of my first lieutenant. She's a nice girl. And she's also engaged herself, to a captain with the 95th Rifle Brigade. But she agreed—" Edward stopped. We were coming out of the woods, now, and the moonlight was bright enough for me to see him push a hand through his hair. "Last year when I was in London—before we were sent over to France, General Powell's wife began to make it clear that she wouldn't be averse to a—"

It was still too dark to be sure, but I thought colour might have crept into Edward's cheeks. "A dalliance with me," he finished. "But besides being an ungentlemanly thing to do, it is also not generally wise to carry on with your commanding officer's spouse. On the other hand, though, she is General Powell's wife. Offend her, and she could make my life a misery for me by speaking a false word in the General's ear: tell him I'd tried to seduce her or was cheating at cards or any other troublemaking lies. Mary Graves and I were friendly. I'd . . . well, I'd done her brother a favour, once, and she was grateful."

"A favour?" I still felt dazed trying to take in everything he said, but I asked, "What did you do?"

"I . . . " Edward rubbed a hand across the back of his neck. "Well, I saved his life for him. At the battle of Rolica, and—why are you laughing?"

The tightness had loosened in my chest, though until he spoke, I had not entirely realised that laughter had bubbled up in its place. "Because that's so like you—because you sound as embarrassed as though you really *had* been caught cheating at cards."

Edward's grin was a quick, rueful flash of white in the dark. "If you're finished mocking me for not wanting to go about boasting of my own heroics, Mary Graves was grateful for what I'd done for her brother. And she agreed to tell Mrs. Powell that she and I were betrothed, so that Mrs. Powell would look for amusement elsewhere." He sobered suddenly, and stopped walking, turning to me to take my hands. "That's the God's honest truth, Georgiana, I swear. I'm not engaged to her or anyone else. Will you—" Edward cleared his throat. "I'm going to try again to say what I wanted to the other day under the oak trees. Will you"—his hands tightened around mine—"Will you promise to at least listen this time? Not run away?"

It seemed as though I could still feel the pressure of Edward's lips against mine, the warmth of his touch flooding through me. "Under the oak trees? Run away?" I repeated.

But Edward had already gone on, speaking more quickly now. "Not that I blame you." Edward shook his head. "I try to tell a girl I'm in love with her and the best I can come up with is to stammer out, 'You know I care about you'? God, I'm an idiot. But I'm going to try to get it right now." He drew a breath and looked down at me. "That night with you, at the Christmas ball—just before I left for France. I couldn't stop thinking about it—about you. I would think about you after battle. Or when we were marching through the heat of summer and men all around me were dropping in their tracks from hunger and disease. But I thought . . . I told myself I was just homesick for England, for Pemberley. What I'd realised I felt for you that night couldn't be real. Because I was still thinking of you as the girl I'd known growing up. I . . . I suppose in my head, I had you frozen around the age of twelve. It seemed wrong to let myself care for you—dream about being with you at night. But then—that first morning I arrived—when I lifted you down from my horse . . . it was like being hit with a bolt of lightning. Realising that I still felt . . . what I felt for you. More strongly, if anything. That it was all real after all."

Edward shook his head again. "I admit it bowled me over. That was why I acted like such a mule with you. I'd made up my mind not to speak—not to say anything. Because here I am, just home from a war, waking up shouting orders to an imaginary regiment at night . . . unable even to stand an evening in company without coming out in a cold sweat and a fit of the shakes. And there Folliet and Carter and all the rest of them were— the kind of men you *ought* to marry, the kind of men you could feel easy about having by your side."

From somewhere in the darkened woods came an owl's low call. Edward stopped and shook his head again. "Even now, I'm not sure I'm doing the right thing in saying this. But I think I have to, or go out of my head." He drew in his breath. His dark gaze was a mixture of longing and trepidation that made my heart feel so full it threatened to spill over. His head bent until his forehead rested against mine, and his hand slid through my loosened hair. His voice was an unsteady murmur. "I love you, Georgiana. I may not be sure of anything else—perhaps not even who I am right now. But I am sure of that."

My throat was so tight I didn't think I'd be able to speak. But I drew back enough that I could raise one hand to touch his face, trace the strong outlines of his brow and temple and cheekbone. I still couldn't quite believe I was not dreaming. But he felt solid and real. The rough stubble on his jaw prickled under my fingertips. "Is this a . . . a proposal of marriage?" I asked.

Some of the light died out of Edward's face at that. He exhaled on a rush of air. "It . . . I wish it were. God knows I want it to be. But I don't see how it can." His hand brushed my hair. "Even if I thought . . . even if I hoped I could persuade you to say yes, I don't . . . trust myself with you. Not the way I am now."

"Because of a few nightmares? Because you don't like to be in crowds?" I looked up at him. "You're still you, Edward. And I trust you. Completely. And as for persuading"—I heard myself laugh, even if it was a mixture of laughter and happy tears—"I've wanted to marry you since I was six years old. I don't think there's a way you could ask me that would lead me to say anything *but* yes."

There was a moment, a heartbeat of stillness, while Edward's eyes looked down into mine. And then his arms were around me and his mouth had settled over mine again.

I don't know how much time had passed—it might have been an hour, even a day—when Edward raised his head. He was breathless again, breathless and shaking, but he put his hands on my shoulders and held me gently away from him. "A year. Give me a year. To put the war behind me, to make myself ready to rejoin the world." He smiled one-sidedly. "I *should* say, to give you a chance to change your mind about being saddled with me for life—but I'm never going to let you, not now."

"You don't have to worry," I whispered.

Edward's arms tightened around me. But he laughed when I kissed him again and turned us both around towards the house. "A year," he said on a ragged exhalation of breath. "Now let's get you back into the house before I lose all control of myself."

That was an hour ago, an hour ago since we parted in the hall outside my room. Edward kissed me again as we stood together at my door and told me to get some sleep if I could. But I'm too happy for that—too happy even now that I've written it all out here. It seems a waste to spend even a moment of this morning asleep.

The sunrise is painting the sky in the east with fiery rose-gold. And soon we'll go downstairs, Edward and I, and speak to my brother. "Your brother may not wish to give his consent," Edward said. "He may think I'm too old for you. Too—"

But I stopped him with a hand across his lips. "Just let Fitzwilliam *try* to refuse," I said.

And Edward laughed. An easier laugh than I had heard from him since he came home.

Even a year of waiting won't seem long. Not when Edward will be there at the end.

DEAR READERS—

Thank you for reading *Georgiana Darcy's Diary*. Georgiana and Edward return in *Pemberley to Waterloo*. If you have enjoyed this book and would like to see more like it, please consider reviewing and/or tagging it on your favorite sites and telling your literary friends about it. Plans for future projects will be based in part on reader feedback and the success of previous projects. It would give me great joy to write what you want to read. If you have found errors or would like to comment privately, I would be grateful for an email at ae@annaelliottbooks.com. Thank you again.

Please visit
www.AnnaElliottBooks.com
for a current list of Anna Elliott titles.

Pemberley to Waterloo

Can their love withstand the trials of war?

GEORGIANA DARCY AND EDWARD FITZWILLIAM want only to be together. But when the former Emperor Napoleon escapes from his exile on the Isle of Elba, Britain is plunged into renewed war with France ... and Edward is once more called away to fight.

To be with the man she loves, Georgiana makes the perilous journey to Brussels, in time to witness the historic downfall of Napoleon at the Battle of Waterloo. But when Edward is gravely injured in the battle, she will need more courage than she ever knew she had to fight for their future together.

Pemberley to Waterloo is the sequel to *Georgiana Darcy's Diary* and is Book 2 of the PRIDE AND PREJUDICE CHRONICLES.

REGENCY TITLES
FROM ANNA ELLIOTT

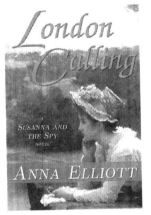

www.AnnaElliottBooks.com

Made in the USA
Lexington, KY
03 November 2012